"Tilghman's first book announces one of the year's most significant debuts . . . filled with surprises, along with a profound sense of place, character, and incident." —*Time*

"Evocative. . . . The mood is deliberate and almost supernaturally calm, even as Tilghman's characters confront decisive moments in their lives with varying mixtures of courage, humor, and resignation."

—Ralph Novak, *People* magazine

"*In a Father's Place* is something new and beautiful in our literature, yet as old as the blood-pull of family love, and the gravity of earth we live on; Tilghman looks behind his characters and under their feet and at their every gesture, to find moral truths; and he is a spiritual writer who often looks at things the rest of us cannot see."   —Andre Dubus

"An accomplished and distinguished collection—one of the best, I'd say, since the heyday of Flannery O'Connor."

—Bruce Allen, *USA Today*

"Tilghman does not evade the most difficult, inevitable subjects, writing about love, death, and faith with the grace and depth of understanding of an unmistakably mature talent. Unlike many first-time authors, his work reflects the confidence and authority of a writer who has found his true material, who is writing about the places, lives, and events that matter to him most. . . . An exceptionally assured literary debut."

—Douglas Seibold, *The Chicago Tribune*

"These are fine stories. Mr. Tilghman writes with penetrating intelligence and with grace about important matters."

—Richard Ford

"Tilghman writes with precision, grace, and an honesty that threatens to topple his astonishingly balanced storytelling."   —Steve Kettman, *San Francisco Chronicle*

"A remarkably mature and significant book . . . plainly one of the strongest fictional debuts in some time."
—Gary Krist, *The Philadelphia Inquirer*

"[*In a Father's Place*] unfolds at a serene pace, the calm born not of detachment but of devoted interest in small details, which open onto larger spaces."
—Ann Hulbert, *The New Republic*

"A superb collection."   —*New York*

"Tilghman's bone-deep knowledge of places—of Montana ranch country and Maryland shore country, of houses and highways—grounds these stories, steadying the fragile insights, the subtle turns in relationships."
—*San Jose Mercury News*

"Tilghman's eloquent stories are works of intelligence, craft, and time. They deal with topics so charged today as to be labeled 'political': patriarchy, abortion, family tradition, class tension, religious belief, and the divine. But they deal with these topics wisely, through art making them transparent for meanings beyond them."
—Thomas D'Evelyn, *The Christian Science Monitor*

"Effectively subdued. . . .Tilghman's stories talk softly but . . . pack a satisfying emotional wallop."
—*The Cleveland Plain Dealer*

"This writer has so long pondered what he has seen and felt, the appropriate words and emotions are of one seamless compact. Here is reading matter. Christopher Tilghman has what it takes, values all that he has, and gives of himself freely."   —Wright Morris

"Tilghman is a writer who does not duck issues or short-change his reader. Each of the seven short stories in his impressive first collection . . . works like a novel in miniature. . . . *In a Father's Place* leaves me impatient to see what he will write next."
—Robert Towers, *The New York Review of Books*

In a Father's Place

IN A
FATHER'S
PLACE

Christopher Tilghman

Picador USA
New York

Picador® is a U.S. registered trademark and is used by St. Martin's Press under license from Pan Books Limited.

Grateful acknowledgment is made to the following, where many of these stories first appeared:
Ploughshares. The New Yorker, The Sewanee Review, The Virginia Quarterly Review.

*The author thanks the following
from the bottom of his heart:
Andre Dubus, Maxine Groffsky,
the Thursday Nighters, Club Swan, and
quarterly editors one and all.
I'm also grateful to
the Massachusetts Council on the Arts and
the Virginia Center for the Creative Arts.*

Library of Congress Cataloging-in-Publication Data
Tilghman, Christopher.
    In a father's place / Christopher Tilghman.
        p.   cm.
    ISBN 0-312-15553-0
    I. Title.
    PS3570.I348I5   1997
    813'.54—dc21   97-7053
                                                            CIP

*First published in the United States of America
by Farrar Straus Giroux*

First Picador USA Edition: May 1997

10   9   8   7   6   5   4   3   2   1

To Caroline

Contents

On the Rivershore

BETWEEN THE CLAY BANKS of the Eastern Shore of Maryland and the brackish waters of the Chesapeake Bay there is a beach a thousand miles long. The sand is fine enough, but it is sharp with oyster shells and rough with stones the color of oxblood and ginger. There's always a tangled line of seaweed running the length of the last high tide. Except for this narrow divider, the rolled farmland and mirrored water meet so seamlessly that on hazy days the big mansions, their pecans and honey locusts like sails, seem to be making their way, somewhere, on the shimmer of the Bay.

On one spot of this beach along the Chester River, there is a boy sitting on the polished curve of a washed-up loblolly pine. His eyes are dry now, but the dirt on his cheeks is streaked and there is salt on his lips. He is holding a crab net and an empty bushel basket, and his broad-brimmed straw hat floats in the water at his feet. Behind him, across a stand of corn beginning to brown in the early August heat, he can hear the steady hum of tractors plowing up an old hay field. Distant on the water he can see seine haulers, waist-deep on the sandbar, setting out the huge net on a necklace of yellow floats. Beyond them the crab boats are painfully bright in the sun, a flash of crystal at the water's edge.

The boy's name is Cecil Mayberry; he is twelve, white, and he knows something. He knows what his mother is going to make for supper, pot roast and green Jell-O salad; he knows that the Russians have put a Sputnik in the sky. But these are not the items that are just now on Cecil's mind. He is thinking about a man, a waterman, lying face down in a tidal pool two hundred yards from where he sits. Cecil knows the man's name, Grayson "Tommie" Todman, and he knows that two .22-caliber bullets have made a mess of Tommie's head. He knows the first one entered just below the right cheekline, cutting short Tommie's last Fuck You to the world, and the second one grazed through his hair before nipping in at the peak and blowing out a portion of Tommie's unlamented brain.

In fact, this is going to be the first time in Cecil's life—but not the last—that he is an undisputed expert on a certain subject. He knows who shot Tommie, and why.

Cecil is just now recognizing that he has to tell someone what he knows. Choosing among his kith and kin, he can think of three people. There is his mother: her birdy face will go taut, she will reach for the hem of her cotton dress to wipe away the sweat along her hair, and then she will run to the barns to fetch his father. Or he can call his sister, Rheta, in town at Tinbutton's Jewelers, and while he waits for her to speak, the greasy barn telephone will glow hot and slippery on his ear. Lastly, he can tell Mr. Matthew McHugh up at the Big House. Cecil cannot remember ever speaking directly to Mr. McHugh, but he has sat patiently in the pickup and listened to the too loud and too quick way his father answers his questions, and he has sensed his father's slowly diminishing pulse of importance as they drive away. Cecil has never been inside the Big House, but he has a fort in the honeysuckle and raspberries out back. He has watched the old man tend his trees—some just the newly planted twigs of slow-growing hardwoods—dragging a red American Boy wagon full of tools as he limps from spot to spot, a dead arm at his side.

Considering all this, even as he wishes it isn't so, there is no real choice to make. He has no idea what Mr. McHugh will do, and that is perhaps the chief reason that he believes Mr. McHugh, alone, can help him. He jumps off his log into the soft water—he's wearing last year's Hi-Tops as crabbing sneakers—and he stoops down to pick up his soggy hat, now fouled with jellyfish tentacles. He places it carefully into his bushel basket, and picks up his crab net. From the water he hears the slow popping of the crab boats, long and white, as they complete a pass and turn for new lines. He's frightened again, and he claws four-legged up the bank, breaking off clumps of clay that are jagged with shells. He runs down to the place where Tommie's body lies hidden in the sharp cordgrass and wedges his basket and net into a marker.

He sets off down the tractor road that cuts through the high corn. He comes to the edge and looks across the flat pastures to the tall red silos and the baking glint of the new aluminum barns. Beyond the far line of lindens that shade the lane he can see the rotating movement of the tractors, his father and Ray Gleason, the farm manager, working as if nothing ever happens on this neck of land. He pauses to reconsider his three choices, and then cuts off the tractor road to follow one of the foul bitter ends of Earle's Cove, past a bee-filled Packard hulk, nose down, a flaring fender lapping in the brine. Where the stream widens into the cove there is a hollow locust tree, and Cecil stops to fight the most forbidden urge to pretend that he'd seen nothing, heard nothing as he crabbed on the rivershore.

Cecil crawls through the last barbed-wire fence and steps onto the foreign land of the Big House, a yellow stucco backdrop through the trees that takes over his horizon. Cecil wipes his sweaty neck; it's so hot that he feels he is rebreathing the same air, over and over; the locusts are already raising a buzz that seems to set the trees on fire. He ducks behind a box bush and studies the three blue doors. He tries to imagine what's behind them, but he can only picture the inside of his own house: a narrow brown entrance hall just wide enough for a man and a flight of stairs, an attached shed where his mother keeps chickens, a gray kitchen with an oilcloth-covered table and four mismatched chairs.

As he knocks on the middle door he wishes he has something to hold, like a basket of eggs or a bag of green tomatoes. The door opens and a large elderly woman fills the frame. It is Henrietta, as round and soft as his mother is hard and flat. She lives in a flaky blue cottage in Niggertown, and he rides in the same school bus with her grandchildren on their way to separate schools. Yes, boy? she says, and there is a milky sound to it. He says he has a message for Mr. McHugh, a message, he says, because he thinks it sounds more important, and then he bursts into tears.

A shiny black arm reaches out the door and gathers him inside, and suddenly he is in a cool place. The coolness surprises him, as if he expected all houses to be stuffy with the dry-lumber heat of his own. He's landed in the kitchen; it looks more like a doctor's office than a place to make supper, but it's reassuring all the same. Henrietta guides him to a chair and then comes at him with a wet dish towel, one large palm around his neck as she washes his face hard, pinching down his nose to clear his nostrils, pulling his eyes wide.

"Now, what's the message?" she asks.

"It's for Mr. McHugh. Just for him."

"Is that a fact," she answers, and leaves Cecil alone in the room. A retriever stirs from the corner and comes over to give Cecil a sniff or two, and Cecil wonders if it can smell the dead man in his head. He sees the first bullet piercing Tommie's snarling cheek and realizes that his last expression as a living human was more like a dog's. Off in the house he hears a clock ticking, a door shut, and a large round laugh. Then he hears the limping walk, a step and a shuffle, of Mr. McHugh. A stroke, that's what his father had told him was wrong with Mr. McHugh, and Cecil wonders, A stroke of what?

Mr. McHugh is standing at the door. He looks tall, but Cecil knows it isn't so; he is wearing tan pants and a white shirt, with a plaid bow tie that is running outside the collar on one side and is pointing almost straight up and down.

"A message for me?" he says.

"I'm Larry Mayberry's boy Cecil and I got something to tell you."

"Hold it, boy. Slow down. Enunciate."

"I'm Larry Mayberry's boy Cecil—"

"Atta boy."

"—and I seen something on the rivershore."

"Haven't been there in years," he says, and Cecil imagines it's true enough. Mr. McHugh turns and waves Cecil to follow. They come out into a hallway with a wide, turning staircase and a wood stove so tall that the nickel urn on top reaches the second-story landing. The floors are covered with smooth straw matting that sings as Cecil scuffs his wet sneakers, and there are pictures everywhere, climbing in sets of four and six, so high that all Cecil can make out at the top is a pile of dead ducks in one and a bright red jacket in another. Cecil wonders if his father has seen this, or if he's ever watched Mr. McHugh turn around backward for the three steps to the porch, holding the rail with his good hand.

"You want something to drink?" he asks as he drops into a wicker chair.

"No." Cecil is busy wondering which of the many chairs he should sit on, or if he should sit at all.

"No, *sir.*"

"No, sir."

"Atta boy."

Cecil decides on a wooden chair with a straight back. He sits facing out, down the sloping lawn with its terraces bordered in box bush and toward the cattails and water elms at the edge of McHugh Creek, toward the water and the faint purple blur of Kent Island far across the river. Through the trees he can see the seine haulers, who have now payed out the net and are closing the trap in a long oval around the sandbar.

"What do you think of trees?"

"I dunno, sir," says Cecil.

"Trees are life. Oxygen. The tree of life. Family trees. All comes back to the soil."

Cecil doesn't understand, so he says, "Tommie Todman's lying dead on the rivershore. He's shot dead."

"Who says?" asks Mr. McHugh.

Cecil is so startled by this question that he snaps back, "I says." He tenses for Mr. McHugh to scold him, but he does not. Instead, he stares at Cecil, and Cecil looks at the way his glasses are sliding on a film of sweat until they are stopped by the splotchy bulb on the end of his nose. A minute, perhaps, has passed, and Cecil begins to wither in this silent heat.

"Two .22-caliber bullets, one in the cheek and one in the head," he adds finally, but he had not planned to tell Mr. McHugh anything except that Tommie was lying there. He did not plan to tell Mr. McHugh, or anyone on God's earth, that he saw the whole thing from behind a root clump of a washed-up pine tree. He did not intend to say anything further because he fears above all the next question: *Who did it?*

"You saw it happen?" Mr. McHugh works himself forward in his chair and his trousers ride up to the silk skin of his calves. Behind him, the long porch, with its red tile and brown ceiling studded with mud-dauber nests, stretches out like a church aisle. "Don't be cagey with me, son."

The word "son" snaps over him like a rifle shot. "I was crabbing on the rivershore," he says, and he thinks even the locusts are suddenly quiet.

"And then?"

Cecil starts to cry again, the third time in three hours, and he tells Mr. McHugh, "Yes, I was there. I was going crabbing on the rivershore and was just coming around the point and I seen Tommie's boat on his trap line—he's always there and he always yells at me for spooking his line—and then I seen someone walking through the cornfield coming toward the shore and he had a gun and I knew this was trouble."

"Who was it?"

"So I was coming around a washed-up pine and I hid behind the root clump, and maybe they already planned to meet, because as soon as Tommie saw him he dropped his line and came over and waded ashore." Tommie wades ashore and the two men start shouting at each other, and Cecil hears Rheta's name, and then his own daddy raises his Remington and squeezes off two .22-longs right into Tommie's head. "Everyone knows Tommie's no good," says Cecil. "He steals from people, he siphons gas from other boats, he gets into fights."

"What happened to the boat?" asks Mr. McHugh. He's sweating so much that Cecil can see gray twisted chest hairs through the damp white shirt.

"It floated off," says Cecil. "I dunno where it went." But that was right—sooner or later someone would find the boat. "I don't want my daddy to go to jail," he says. He tells Mr. McHugh he had to come tell someone, because even if the buzzards eat Tommie clean up and no one cares or misses him ever, he knows his daddy, and sooner or later, after milking is done today probably, he's going to walk into Officer Stapleton's office and turn himself in.

Cecil is now going to say something about his mom, and Rheta, and about their dogs, Dusty and Blackie, and their house at the end of the farm that has been his whole life and has been his mom's whole life because she was born in the back bedroom . . . but Mr. McHugh raises a spotted hand and shushes him short.

"Help me up," he says, and Cecil goes to grab a bony hand and pulls him up with so little effort that he wonders why Mr. McHugh asked for help in the first place. Mr. McHugh does not drop his hand before he says, "Now stop worrying. You sit here. Henrietta will bring you a sandwich."

Cecil waits in his chair. At the very top of the tallest pecan tree there is a slight rustle of wind that brings with it the moist smells of the cows, and he thinks of tails slimy with manure. He thinks of Tommie saying Fuck You, but it was the sharp report of the rifle that echoed out onto the water, far out over the sandbars of the seiners and the narrows where the watermen were digging at the rivers. In the hush he pictures Tommie Todman stirring, hunching to all fours and wiping the gore from his head as if it were a clot of seaweed, and leaning back on his haunches in front of that small pool while he rubs his temples to clear his sight. Keep away from the watermen, his father had told him, but Cecil didn't know why. Charky James and Mike Ferguson, their fathers were watermen, and they came to school night in their white shirts and creased green chinos just like his dad, and just like his dad their skin was brown and scarred and flaky except for a line on their foreheads, up where the sun never reached, that was puffy and white, just like the skin under a Band-Aid or the nose of a newborn calf.

He hears a car approaching, and for a moment he

thinks it is Officer Stapleton, but he hears the high yelp
of Ray Gleason's beagles. Henrietta opens the big door
and Cecil hears Ray and Mr. McHugh talking and, in
between, the muffled, beaten sound of his father's
voice. He waits, and Henrietta comes out with a sandwich and a glass of milk. It is the hottest and stillest
part of the day, when the sound of a lone heron shifting
feet lingers in the air. He is sharpened to it, tensed for
the noise in the rooms behind him, waiting for his
father's footsteps, but when the door opens again, it is
Mr. McHugh backing down the steps, holding a bright
yellow life preserver over his arm.

Mr. McHugh catches his breath for a moment, and
Cecil hears Ray's truck, with its bodyguard of beagles,
drawing back to the farm. Mr. McHugh turns to him.
"What we're going to do now is wrong by every standard but one. You better remember that, all your life,
if that's what it takes."

"Yes, sir."

"It's history. History's *our* judge, boy. Do you
understand?"

"No, sir."

"Atta boy. Now help me put this thing on." He holds
out the life jacket. Cecil fumbles a bit before he guides
the limp arm through the hole and buckles the three
web ties in front, and then realizes that there are also
two long straps that come from the back and must be
looped through the legs, and he hesitates. "Come on.
Tie me up. I'm not going to sink, no matter what."

So Cecil kneels directly in front of Mr. McHugh and

reaches through his thighs for a strap, and guides it along the leg and tightens it well. He does it again on the other side, this time encountering the spongy resistance of his crotch. When he is done Mr. McHugh tries each strap and is satisfied, and he points out the screen door and toward the creek. They make their way down the corridor of box bushes, and Mr. McHugh leans so hard on every other step that Cecil feels what it is like to be lame.

When they come out of the narrow path through the cattails and creek grass, Cecil sees Ray and his father pacing at the end of the dock. The farm's aluminum duck boat is tied alongside and it booms as it nudges the creosoted pilings. His father won't look him in the eye, rushing to load Mr. McHugh into the center seat, but once they have pushed off and Ray has brought the small outboard up to speed, Cecil feels an arm coming around him and gathering him in. Even in the breeze Cecil can smell the sour milk and manure and sweat of the farmer. Cec? his father shouts into Cecil's ear. Yes, Daddy, Cecil answers. Cec, his father says again, and they ride like this with the water crackling against the metal hull and the long wake stretching from side to side in the creek, as if it were taking the measure of this marshy little inlet before it became lost on the bay.

Cecil sees ten cement blocks stowed in the center in front of Ray, and a green tarp, a toolbox, and a spool of new chain. As soon as he realized they were going out on the water he knew what Mr. McHugh had decided to do with Tommie's body, out in the deep channel of the river a mile from shore on either side, and he's so glad that it doesn't matter he's sure it can't work. He looks at the brilliant roll of new chain, wound in a perfect repeating pattern of links, and still cannot believe they will throw it over the side, with or without Tommie's body attached. Cecil is worried that Ray will change his mind at the last minute, and he lowers his eyes to watch as the fresh manure and turned earth still wedged into his father's boot soles make whorls in the clear rainwater on the boat bottom.

The water picks up a slight chop as they round the point in the river, swinging wide by hundreds of yards, yet still in barely two feet of water. The seine haulers are hard at it, too busy with a net of frothy water to notice the farmers. Cecil runs his eye up the shining line of sand, but he cannot yet see the high weeds of the duck pond or the marker he made with his net and basket. His father is fighting against the growing swell, and Mr. McHugh is holding on tight with his good hand.

"Do you see it?" Ray yells.

Cecil shouts back, "Not yet. Halfway down maybe." Then he realizes with a jolt that his father knows where Tommie is, knows better than he does. But Ray lets Cecil's answer stand, and they push on, past the five posts that are all Hurricane Carol left of a duck blind, past a floating island of water celery and seaweed.

"There," yells his father, and he reaches a long arm out to point with a lack of shame that catches Cecil by surprise. But Cecil sees his father is at work now—whatever the circumstances, he'll do his job.

Ray slows the engine and heads in, cutting all power as they guide around the root clump and come to a stop with a gentle scrape a few feet from the beach. Cecil's father, still in his newest pair of leather boots, jumps out and heads around the clump of cattails, and Cecil runs to catch up, perhaps to see if all his most fervent wishes, for a miracle of God or fast work of the buzzards, have removed the body from the earth. But it is still there; as they approach there is a white scattering of crabs from the half-submerged head. His father stops, makes a confused and nauseous coughing sound, but there is no help for it, it's bad work, and when Ray comes up they each grab a leg and pull the body full onto the sand.

It's the mouth. That's what Milly Richardson's dad, who was a medic in France, said makes the dead scary. Even if their face is blowed off, he said, there's still a mouth, a mouth they spat from or ate through just minutes before they died. Fuck You was the last thing through Tommie's mouth. Cecil can see it still on those yellow teeth, on a tongue that is now swollen and milk-white; he sees it still on the pierced and broken side of the face and skull that the crabs have picked into long strings of scalp and skin. Then Cecil goes to the cattails and throws up, splattering a clear powerful burst of vomit through the serrated leaves.

When he recovers and looks back, his father and Ray have wrapped the tarp tight around the body, and

Ray is putting his full weight against the chain as his father works to catch the tightest link around the waist with a grab hook. They do the same around the neck and feet, cutting off a good length each time with bolt cutters, working smoothly together as if they're trying to thread a control wire through the guts of a combine. Cecil has always thought of his father that way—he will for the rest of his life: ready to catch or snag or tighten something Ray's feeding to him, never the boss, but always the first one the boss picks. Cecil has taken pride in that, but it seems wrong, today, for Ray to take charge. Cecil wants to hear his daddy say, This is my problem, Ray, I'll take care of it, or, You go on back to the boat. Cec and me'll bring him around.

They carry the body to the boat. There's no way to cover the head end, clearly a human skull even through the tarp, sticking up over the gunwale. Mr. McHugh hasn't moved, held up maybe by the tight padding of the jacket, and though Cecil is grateful beyond reckoning for the decision Mr. McHugh has made, he can't avoid the beginning of the belief that Mr. McHugh, in some way, caused it all to happen in the first place.

Cecil pushes them off into the slight chop, now a gentle roll pushed by a freshened breeze. The gulls are out again; the sounds from the long white crab boats are deliberate now, a more purposeful mechanical hum in the place of the drowsy popping of the diesels. They have now passed through the midday heat that seems to make a cover for men on the Bay, and are entering the sharp western sun that casts long shadows behind everything that moves. Cecil looks back to see how far they've come, and sees Mr. McHugh with his lower lip hanging open, the skin inside pink and wet. His father is working over the body, feeding the chains through three blocks at a time and closing the loops with repair links; two times the soft pin falls out just as he's ready to crimp it with pliers, and he swears. Then Cecil looks at Ray at the outboard, and sees panic on his face.

He whips his head forward and realizes immediately that one of the crab boats has broken loose and seems to be heading toward them. Just to Queenstown, he tells himself, just going to the crab shacks. But it isn't true; the boat is up to full speed and is carving a wide arc to intercept them. Throw him over now! he wants to yell, but he knows it's still too shallow and the body, weighted down with all its chains and blocks, would be impossible to move quickly. His father looks like a mask, a frozen face with wild eyes.

"I think it's Avery Miller," yells Ray, and Cecil does not know if that means anything, anything more than a wave when you pass on the road to town.

"Do you know him?" croaks Mr. McHugh.

Ray shrugs. Cecil can see the man clearly now, standing in his deckhouse and leaning as the boat banks off course. He's in waders that make him look like two halves of the wrong man, and he is holding a red megaphone, a long cone that explodes his face at the mouth. "Yo," he yells. Ray cuts the engine; it's over now. Cecil can imagine what they look like to the waterman, so lost and out of place on the river that they might simply have taken a wrong turn at the old elm.

"We're looking for Tommie Todman," Avery Miller yells, but all at once he drops the megaphone to his side, opens his mouth to the roundest O Cecil has ever seen, and stares in wonder. "What in hell?" he says.

The two boats rise and fall, twenty feet apart. And then, suddenly panicked, the waterman jumps for his air horn and gives out six short blasts that break into the air cleanly, petrels swooping low and fast above the swells. As the sound slowly dies, it seems as if nothing will come of it, but then, a mile away in the Narrows, there is an instant response from the other boat as nets are dropped heedlessly on the deck and the engine powers to life.

"This isn't your concern, Miller," says Ray. "Just keep away."

"What in hell," Miller repeats. He's pacing back and forth on the low, broad fantail.

"He ain't worth it to any of us. You know that as well as me," says Ray.

Cecil is waiting for Mr. McHugh to explain. When he finally speaks, he says, "This isn't a simple thing, boys."

But Avery Miller pays no attention to Mr. McHugh. "Who did it?" he asks Ray.

Ray begins to refuse an answer, but his father won't allow it. "I done it," he says. "For five years I told him to keep away from my Rheta, but he wouldn't stop. She can't go anywhere without him following. Wouldn't listen to her saying no. Didn't care. Now he's saying if Rheta won't go with him, he'll . . . well, it ain't for you to know that. Five years is enough, is all. So I told him to meet me on the rivershore."

Ray says, "Now you know it's true. You know what Larry says is God's truth. Tommie's got no family and no one gives a pig's ass for what happens to him."

The other boat has approached close enough to cut speed, and as it breaks into a wide banking turn, Cecil sees that the driver is Morris James, Charky's daddy, and Charky is there alongside his father, looking scared. Morris James is holding a rifle, and he yells over to the waterman, "The farmers killed him? Is that Tommie? Holy Christ."

"That's the smart of it," says Avery, trying to sound sure in front of his fellow waterman, but he's still so shaken his voice breaks into a dry croak. "The crazy son-of-a-bitch went too far this time."

That's right, says Cecil to himself, the crazy son-of-a-bitch. And there they bob for a moment or two, the duck boat, the *Mrs. Avery Miller*, and the *Wendy B. Honey*. Far down the channel, buoy number 6 clangs dully, marking the way toward open water. The aluminum boat catches the side of the crab boat and then comes free with a jolt against the swell that makes the corpse settle slightly. Cecil is afraid his father will get seasick.

"You was going to get him wet?" asks Morris James.

"We're going to throw him over, if that's what you mean. And why the hell not?" yells Ray. "Just keep away, goddamn you."

Cecil feels as if the voices are flying all over the river. Mr. McHugh says, "Hold it. Slow down. Think clearly."

"You keep out of this, Mr. McHugh," says Morris. "You keep your thinking to yourself."

"Grab the line and let's tow them in," says Avery, high and fevered. "What are we waiting for?"

Mr. McHugh takes out a handkerchief and washes the spray from his face, and then Cecil understands he's trying to get up, locking his bad leg at the knee and wedging it against the flotation tank. It's not working, Cecil says to himself; the others simply watch as the old man struggles upright, like an old cow. Finally on his feet, Mr. McHugh looks at the watermen to either side and says, "What we're doing is wrong by every standard but one. It's history . . ." but before he can go any further a swell builds from under Avery Miller's boat and catches the duck boat broadside and sends Mr. McHugh backward, full weight and free fall across the seat, and if it hadn't been for the high padded collar of the life jacket his head would have hit the aluminum with nothing to slow it down but the hard knock of metal. Cecil leaps forward to help, but Mr. McHugh waves him away as he jerkily rights himself, drooling and panting, on the bottom of the boat.

"You shut him up, Ray," Avery Miller screams

again, and Cecil sees now that the waterman is losing control of himself, full force into panic. "By Jesus, that bastard ain't going to be the one to solve this."

"Stop worrying about McHugh," Morris replies quickly in an even tone. "Tommie's the problem here."

"Ain't no one gonna kill a waterman," says Avery, and Cecil knows he's said what everyone is thinking. He knows Morris James, or even his best friend, Charky, can't argue against what everyone, on and off the water, has been saying for generations. Cecil figures they're lost; his daddy's gone. The boats have drifted slightly apart now; they've long since passed the mouth of McHugh Creek and they're moving around Hail Point toward the Bay itself.

"It ain't a waterman I killed," says Cecil's father quietly. "It ain't nobody but a son-of-a-bitch who figured my girl was his special joke. He figured I couldn't do nothing just because he *was* a waterman, but that's my joke on him, because I knew he was just a son-of-a-bitch. I'm done with him now and I'm done with this. So pull us in."

Cecil shifts on the hard aluminum seat and drops his hand into the warm waters of the river. Finally, Morris James says, "Why buy the water when the fish are free, Avery? That's my point. How did you feel, nights, when you and Tommie was the only ones left at the landing? Sooner or later . . ."

"It speaks of trouble to me," says Avery, but he's calmer now. "Right smart of trouble."

"Since when ain't it? We've had nothing but trouble ever since Tommie's been out here."

"No one kills a waterman," Avery repeats. It's the thing that makes the best sense to him.

"Oh hell, in two years' time he'd be pumping gas, at the rate he was going. Or dead. I got my boy to think about."

Ray Gleason hasn't said a thing for a long time, but he's a family man and speaks from the heart. "Larry's boy's here too. The boys is the issue. Not us."

They're over the deep: a hundred feet, two hundred; it's enough, more than enough.

"It ain't just the boys," says Morris James. "It's the water. We got to think what's best for the water. Who's gonna follow the water after we swallow the anchor, Avery? Kids like Tommie Todman?"

The two watermen stand, staring into each other. Avery shakes his head once, and Morris gathers Charky into his side. From way back at Carpenter's Island Cecil hears the big engine of the seine haulers come to life, and he wonders if the five men who worked so hard all day are going home looking at bins only half full of perch and rock. Farther behind he imagines he can hear the bellows of the cows, lined up with full udders while the new hand, Bobbie, scratches his head, wondering if he should go looking for the others under an overturned tractor. Cecil figures it's the same at the landing when the boats are late; the water can hurt these men. None of them can swim, that's code, just like it's code when a waterman dies they take his boat out and sink it, and sooner or later a half-submerged wreck finds its way nose up in the grass and weeds.

"You got them chains on good, Ray?" asks Morris James.

Ray nods, and doesn't even wait a second more before he begins to push the blocks over the side. Cecil's father is right alongside him in a flash and they move Mr. McHugh—Cecil's forgotten about him—to one side. They wedge two oars under the body and pry it up with the heavy blocks doing most of the work. It catches on the gunwale for a second, but then breaks free with a clatter of chains on the aluminum and sinks down into the deep, tea-colored waters of the Chesapeake Bay.

The watermen stay to watch the body sink, but no one says anything more, and when it's gone they start up their engines and head for home. Charky turns and gives Cecil a small wave, and the two boys watch each other from their fathers' sides. Cecil stares at the boats with their long sterns deep into frothy troughs, driving hard for Queenstown, a distant water tower above the crab shacks. Over the water tower, behind Kent Island, rises the still-new steel lattice of the Chesapeake Bay Bridge, a wonder of the world that goes clear to Annapolis. And the boats, now dark dots in the low afternoon sun, are driving for it because it marks home, and Cecil wonders what Charky's house looks like, what his mother is cooking right now, and if his daddy ever sings to him at night. He leans into his own father's arm, but it's not the same warm side he has slept against in the car on the way home from the pictures. Suddenly he wishes he'd waved back at Charky, or said something to him, and he wonders if, at night, Charky ever wakes up scared, if he's ever asked himself what it's for, living here on this land just barely afloat on fragile banks of clay and sand.

And almost thirty years later, after Mr. McHugh has died and Ray has retired and the cows are gone and the corn land is leased out to a grain conglomerate, and after Avery Miller has died and Charky comes home from Vietnam changed forever, and the catch is down and the oystermen go to war with the clam diggers and the seine haulers give up for good, Cecil Mayberry brings his three children for a walk along the rivershore. They're all in funeral clothes, and after the walk he and Rheta will pack up their mother to move in with her sister Gladys. His boy and two girls, who've grown up in a Baltimore suburb, run down the rocky beach toward the rounded point that is the only remaining sign of the old duck pond. Cecil watches them stop to pick up bright pieces of plastic flotsam, and the boy holds up a pink tricycle wheel with a hoot, and then they're gone, deep into the cattails and cordgrass.

Loose Reins

THEY DROVE WEST out of Gallatin Field just after seven when the cool air from the mountains began to slide across the hot rooftops of Bozeman and the crackling brush of the plains. Between the smudgy morning sun of Boston and the tinder light of Montana's late afternoon they had spent eleven hours in three airplanes, and in three more hours they would be standing in front of Hal's mother. In the airport men's room Hal had changed from his business suit to jeans, and while he rented a car, Marcie sat on a curb and watched goats as they chewed slowly through the iron grasses at the airport entrance.

"You've got to understand," he said after they had settled well into the drive, "some of them are college graduates; some of them are murderers. You never know which and you never try to guess."

"But not Roy," she said.

" 'Not Roy' what?"

"Well, not a college graduate or a murderer. I thought Roy was just a drunk."

"*All* hay hands are drunks. Otherwise, why would they live the way they do?"

"I don't know, Hal," she answered quickly. She turned her thin face away from him and out into the darkness, at the solitary yard lights beginning to glow on the mottled flatlands. He glanced at the speedometer and slowed, remembering what his father had said to him years ago: At night, watch out for the whiteface when they come onto the road to stand in the heat.

"It shouldn't surprise us," said Marcie. "What else was she going to do?"

Hal let out a long groan, and she reached over to pat him on the shoulder. She let her hand stay there, a touch, after nearly twenty years together, that said, Easy, easy. She had been saying that, one way or another, for a day and a half. She had called him at the bank, saying, "Now take it easy, but you won't believe this letter we just got from your mother," and an hour later he had rescheduled a Lending Committee meeting, had broken three appointments and left his secretary to make excuses. It was unwise to move so fast, but the news that his mother had married Roy—not that she was planning to, but that she had already done it in the dim gray light of an empty courtroom with Miss McAvoy, his old spelling teacher, as a last-minute witness—had found and gripped the child within Hal like a ring through his nose.

"I should think it's funny," he said.

"No. Not funny."

"Well, then droll."

The air outside was cool now, rich with the smells of cattle and sage. Far ahead a bolt of heat lightning backlit a tall ridge, a long and craggy shape Hal had learned from his bedroom window like a nursery rhyme. A half hour later he caught the first faint lights of Millersburg, the thin thread of a town starting high at the old silver mine, dropping down past Gannon's Department Store and the neon thrills of the Four Aces, past the bermed-up field where the high school played six-man football, and ending on the flat with Peltzer's Feed and Seed and Fetchko's Allis-Chalmers Sales and Service.

"There it is," he said.

Marcie was dozing. There it is, he repeated to himself. Two years ago in the spring he had come back to bury his father, and he had expected his mother would soon begin the process of returning East. But she had stayed, a rancher's widow now despite a childhood in Philadelphia and a college degree from Bryn Mawr. She hired up one extra for haying and finished the summer season. Then she hired one more for wintering and spring calving. "I guess after forty-five years this damn state's become home to me," she said when Hal called her in May to wish her happy birthday. "I guess I think what's done with cattle makes the best sense for me."

He shook Marcie's thigh as they pulled off the state road onto the yellow dust of Easy Street. They turned again at a green mailbox full of bullet holes, dipped down across Dunning Creek, with its low lace of scrubby aspens and water oaks, and as the car headed up the other side, the headlights caught her, standing in front of the dark log house, her long gray hair wrapped in its bun, the tails of her yellow shirt out, as always, over her wide hips. A dog Hal didn't know sat at her feet.

"So you've come," she said, turning slightly away from Hal's hand left too long in the middle of her back.

Marcie walked forward and gave her a hug.

"Well," said Hal, "we couldn't let this pass without a celebration."

"This is very sweet of you."

He nodded vigorously to say, Sweet, but the least we could do, and began to move onto further rehearsed lines. But over her shoulder he saw Roy, standing back just out of the light, midway between the driveway and the house. He was thinner now, almost gaunt, with his baggy blue jeans gathered at the waist by a web belt and scratched brass army buckle. He had a gray stubble of hair setting off his big ears, the only part of him that didn't look beaten and malnourished. He stood with his arms hanging at his side, self-contained and beyond permanent judgment, as he must have done all those years when the ranchers sized him up for a place in a hay crew, a job digging potatoes, piecework picking raspberries or a winter pruning grapes.

Hal walked around his mother and stepped over to him. "Roy! I guess this is congratulations."

Roy took his hand loosely. "Hal," he said, and took one step back.

It's Roy, all right, thought Hal as he noticed that Roy now had a new set of teeth, uppers and lowers. He called Marcie over, hearing himself using the *bonhomie* of the cocktail party or museum show opening.

"A pleasure," said Roy to Marcie, adding "ma'am." As he said it, he was staring straight at Jean. Without saying anything further he grabbed the two suitcases Hal had unloaded and shuffled into the house.

They all stood for a moment watching him go. Jean said, "Roy gets real cold these days."

Hal was still trying to pump festivity into the air. He said, "So you're married now. Newlyweds."

"Oh, Hal, what a tawdry thing to say." It came out quickly, and just as quickly she followed it with a short laugh, as if they knew it had been a joke all along. "You park," she said. "Marcie and I will make tea."

He moved the car over alongside the old blue International pickup that in town, or in the haylands, or in the streets of Butte or Anaconda had always meant his father was near. He stood for a moment in the black light of the ranch yard, feeling the smooth brush of the anthracite air that returned on the cusp of Montana's harvest moon. It was the season for preparation, and for Hal, year after year, that had meant leaving for boarding school like the last of the hay hands walking out to thumb a ride on Easy Street, leaving for college, leaving for Marcie Donnelly, always back East.

"You didn't go check on the horses," Jean said when he came in. She turned to Marcie; Roy was nowhere. "Both of them used to do that every time they came back. We'd see the light go on."

"It's too cold."

Marcie was sitting at the straw-colored Formica table, now back to family size. In hay season it formed a long oblong, surrounded by a hunched crew of men smelling of grass and work and saying "ma'am" and "boy" to the family, but never saying anything to Hal's father seated at the head. There wouldn't have been much point; he used to pass every meal staring out the picture window for rain clouds. And at his right hand— Hal could see it now—sat Roy, so incapacitated with DTs during his first few weeks back that he had to lean into his coffee and slurp like a dog.

Jean continued, "Fred always said they didn't trust us to take care of the horses. Or the ranch, for that matter. As if anything ever changes around here." She was leaning against one of the two stoves in the kitchen part of the room.

"What I was trying to say outside before you dismissed me was that we're happy for you. That's the main thing."

34

"Thank you."

"But . . ." he stammered. "I can't say it wasn't a bit of a shock. Am I allowed to say that?"

"Of course. You can say whatever you want. Of course it was a shock. Mark sent me an awful card with one of those sticky poems about 'the most important day of your life,' and all he wrote on it was an exclamation point. It was killing."

So, thought Hal, if she sent a letter to Mark in Denver and he had already returned a card, she must have told Mark first. "Mark always did know how to make you laugh."

"Now, Hal, don't be adolescent. The thought of coming to visit would never even occur to Mark. You know that. He's probably forgotten the whole thing by now."

She walked out of the kitchen and into the mudroom, and Hal could soon hear the thuds of frozen meat as she hunted through the old Kelvinator chest freezer. He shrugged at Marcie. "Be nicer," she whispered. He looked around at the shapes in the dark, the pile of county *Stockmen's News* back issues on the counter behind the table, a line of feed-store ball caps hung on pegs, the laundry wall tinseled with school rodeo ribbons won mostly by Mark.

"Sit down," said Marcie. "Have some tea."

"I'll take the suitcases up. I'm tired."

They heard a hollow shout from the center of the freezer: "In Mark's room. Roy snores."

Hal was groggy, fighting dizzying flashes of sleep.

He rolled his eyes one last time for Marcie, and trudged off into his boyhood home. Upstairs, he stripped in the chilly air and crawled into one of the twin beds, amid the airplane models, horse posters, and framed school diplomas of his younger brother. In his prayers he remembered his daughters, six and eight years old, especially the younger, Sarah, who'd just gotten glasses and was miserable, and he tried to imagine his own father, and whether his father had ever prayed for him.

Hal woke up about seven, early enough to slip out without waking Marcie, and late enough to find the kitchen empty. His mother's car was gone. He'd reclaimed an old, broken pair of boots, and a wide belt with *Buckwood* spelled out in silver. He ate his cold cereal looking out at the mowed haylands, their new orange shoots of alfalfa and timothy brushed with frost.

All those dewy early mornings, Roy used to slink over from the bunkhouse, surly and crow-eyed, his tin cup in his hands. In later years, after no one could argue with his seniority, he took up the lead each day in front of a snickering pack of hay hands, and when breakfast was done he stayed on for a last cup of coffee, a privilege no other hay hand had ever tried to assume. And there he would be when the boys came down, like a deaf uncle that no one liked but everyone had learned not to notice.

Hal was six or seven the day Roy first showed up from nowhere, like all of them, to ask for work, and even though those drifters used to frighten him, there was something comical about this one, such a skinny teenager, his enormous ears holding up a big black hat. He tried to sound cocky, but his voice was weak with hunger. Fred put him on the stacking crew. In those days, they stacked hay loose with beaverslides, and two men worked underneath to distribute the loads evenly out to the backstop and wings. It was only after they had made their painful way up toward the top of the cone that the breezes blew the chaff out of their eyes and their mouths. Often rattlesnakes would come in with the load, but they were almost always too dazed from their dusty flight to make anything more than a feeble coil before being clubbed with a shovel kept handy for the purpose.

Usually the men of the stacking crew lasted only a single season, and even if they came back again, Fred put them on the buckrakes. But he kept putting Roy back under the beaverslide, and Roy never complained, just took the tin cup of water and drank, and gave it back, no expression on those clean lips or in those red, watery eyes. Mark and Hal spent their summers at the edges of haying, staying out of their father's way as they chased the badgers and skunks that had been routed—usually maimed—by the mowers. Even then Mark had a careless manner, a kind of neglect that made him a favorite with the hay crew. They called him "Markie," and all through those summers when Roy was in the stacks Hal would glance across the freshly mowed haylands to see Mark hanging on the bars, talking, passing the time, like a wife visiting the jails.

Hal poured himself a second cup of coffee, and looked out the window across the ranch yard. He heard a loud clang from the equipment shed and saw the electric blue snap of the welder sparking deep in the shadows. He thumbed through an issue of the *News*, paused over the latest quotes from Chicago, but when Marcie came down he'd given up reading and was staring out the window up the creek valley toward the Pintlar Peaks. She was carrying the present she'd insisted on buying during the mad rush out of Boston, and slid the silver-and-blue package into the center of the table.

"Is everything okay?" she asked.

"Sure. Of course."

She hunted through the cabinets for bread. Out of the corner of his eye she looked like all those Millersburg girls, midway between babysitting and town jobs, who had come to work for Jean during haying. What had happened to those girls, Dawn, Rae, Sandy, and Jill? When Hal's mother wasn't looking some of them used to flirt with the hands, and one year one of them—Hal couldn't just now remember her name—took a shine to Roy. She must have thought Roy a catch, a cowboy with his own bunkhouse, and a few times in the fall she drove up in an old Ford. Jean shooed her away when she saw her, but still they passed a few Sunday afternoons together, and maybe one or two evenings. By then, Roy had finally made his way off the stack. He'd begun to stay on as the ranch hand, sometimes straight through the winter. He had a fair way with the cattle and could be trusted when there was real trouble afoot, but most of the time he did only what Fred bullied and shamed him into.

"She said she figured you'd wait until the weekend before you came and you would have time to think things over if her letter arrived on Monday or Tuesday. That's why she sent your letter later than Mark's." Marcie sat down with her coffee and English muffin.

"She always knew how to manipulate us."

"Frankly, I don't think manipulating you is high on her agenda these days."

After she ate her breakfast Marcie went outside. Hal had finally decided to stir from his seat when he heard the rattle of the Ford station wagon as it pounded over the bridge and came into view with its own cloud of dust. Jean appeared, carrying a yellow three-ring binder bulging with section dividers. She wished him good morning as she came through the kitchen on the way to her slant-top desk, and asked him to come to town with her in a few minutes to pick up a tractor being rebuilt at Fetchko's. Soon she was on the telephone arguing loudly about a pro-rated guarantee on asphalt shingles. "That's crap," he heard her say.

He followed Marcie out onto what his mother still called the veranda. There were two redwood chaises, the kind with wooden wheels, and Hal remembered sometimes looking down from his bedroom during the day and catching her sitting there, looking blankly off at the jagged horizon. He could see her arms lying dead at her sides, her feet veering out, and each time she moved it was with a great heaving breath. Often Hal watched until Mark, fluid and slack, found her there. He would place himself in front of her like a stand-up comic, forcing her gaze away from the mountains, and in a few minutes Hal would hear her laugh before getting up to make supper.

"Doesn't Marcie look pretty there," said his mother as they met beside the car. Hal glanced over and saw the shine of her auburn hair over the top of the chaise.

"She's gotten so much prettier now that she's older," his mother went on, placing herself squarely, heavily, in the driver's seat. As soon as they had turned on Easy Street, she announced, "There is perhaps one more thing you should know. There's no sex between us."

"Good God," said Hal.

"Not that you have a right to know or care, but it seems something worth clearing up."

"Not that I *want* to know or care." He looked out at the fence posts flashing by like newsreel frames. "But what is it, then? Can you imagine what it's going to be like during the winter?"

"Of course we talk, most of the time about—"

Hal interrupted. "You tell him all about the 1937 Cotillion and he tells you about squeezing Sterno in Missoula."

"Is that a joke, dear?"

Hal shrugged and then dismissed his comment, but

she did not take up the conversation again. She let him ride in silence as they finished the climb out of the small creek valley and onto the flat, a smooth plain over to the ridge, where the buildings of Millersburg gathered around a fissure like a black tangle of bees.

"I'm trying to understand," he said.

"Understand this, then. I'm twenty-six years ahead of you. You can pass judgment on your father now, but not on me. You'll have plenty of time for that when I'm dead and gone."

"I'm not attacking you."

"I'm not saying you are. If I thought so, you'd be on the shoulder walking home right now, just like the last time you sassed me."

"That was Mark."

"Was it? God, your father was mad at me for that."

They were entering town, past the large, mostly blank sign that announced, "You can still see Millersburg" to the state road. They pulled into Allen Fetchko's, drove around to the back of the windowless tin building, and stopped outside the black hole of an equipment bay. Hal began to get out, but she leaned her head out the window and bellowed Allen's name into the darkness. Hal heard the thud of a dropped tire, and a moment later Allen came out, as always wearing a short-sleeved white shirt and orange tie, with green axle grease right up to his elbows.

He greeted Hal with a surprised look, but gave him the guarded smile of the small-town tradesman who knows every ranching operation within fifty miles. Hal followed him over to the tractor, a piece of machinery that had bedeviled his father for the last four years of his life.

"How many times are we going to rebuild this thing?" asked Hal, climbing into the seat.

"Tell Roy to break it in real easy this time."

"You better deliver the message yourself," said Hal.

Allen wiped a spot of grease off his tie and said patiently, "Not above twelve hundred for the first fifty hours."

Hal kicked over the starter, and both of them waited for the engine to catch.

"I guess I should be saying congratulations," said Allen.

Hal frowned.

"Oh, don't pick a fight with Roy."

"He wouldn't notice if I did."

Allen dropped back a pace or two, trying to frame all of Hal in his sight. "Now look here, Hal. It seems to me you boys ought to be a little grateful."

Hal knew he was losing control over nothing with exactly the wrong person, but it felt too good to stop. "Does it?" he hissed. "Does it seem that way to you?"

Allen Fetchko shook his head, as if he had just heard wrong; he was accustomed to the last word. "We all figured one of you would come home and do the right thing. Of course it seemed a whole lot more likely that it would be Mark."

At that, Hal popped the clutch and jackrabbited forward. Stones, sand, and gravel fired backward, hitting something metallic with a deep, penetrating *sluggg* and, from Allen, a murderous *Heyyy!* Hal took off with a rubbery clatter of tire lugs and stinging vibrations traveling up his legs, and it wasn't until he reached the Millersburg sign that he looked at the tachometer and remembered that this time they were supposed to break it in easy.

When Hal came into the kitchen he found the three of them sitting, staring at the silver-foil-wrapped present on the table. Roy gazed at the unfamiliar thing with a watchful eye and was plainly excited and eager to get started. Hal went immediately to the laundry room to wash, and cleaned his hands right down to the fingertips. He listened for sounds of unwrapping, but they still waited for him, and it wasn't until he had settled into the fourth chair that Roy finally reached forward to gather the box into his rough hands. He trembled slightly, handling the paper too gently, and when he had gotten down to the box he hesitated for a moment, as if this was something he was expected to do.

This drove Jean beyond the narrow limits of her patience. "Oh, Roy. Please *do* go ahead."

He took the lid off and parted the tissue, and brought out a crystal bowl. Hal had forgotten what it was. Roy said nothing, but went over to the window and turned the bowl in the sun, its facets deep and brilliant. The room filled with color. Finally, he turned and sat again. "I've never seen anything so clear. I've never seen nothing so pretty that I can hold in my hands."

Marcie beamed and glanced reproachfully at both Hal and his mother.

"It's like mountain water. It's not like any glass I ever saw."

Jean said, "Waterford. How very nice of you."

"Marcie picked it out," said Hal, wondering how in God's name she knew how to do it. What does he like? she had asked. Does he read or play games? How the hell do I know, he snapped back, and he fumed in rage when she told the cabdriver to swing by Shreve's on the way to the airport.

Roy said to Jean, "Do you do something special with a bowl like this? Is it for something?"

"For whatever we want," she answered.

He picked it up one last time and carried it carefully over to the counter, where it could sit in full sunlight. He went back to his place, but remained standing as if, Hal thought, he planned to give a toast. He said, "That's a real fine present," and Hal thought that would be all until, so quick he almost might not have noticed or believed it, Roy gave him a short, dignified bow.

Jean passed out sandwiches and Kool-Aid.

Marcie said, "We're going to Anaconda this afternoon."

"But I thought we were going for a ride," said Hal.

Jean said, "There's a girl in Andaconda who dyes and weaves her own wool. I've promised Marcie a skirt."

In spite of everything, Hal nearly burst out laughing,

hearing his mother, after all these years, referring to the place as An*d*aconda like everyone else. He waved the three of them off in the station wagon with a jolly smile, but the cheer was gone by the time he caught Chief in the corral, and he forced himself to whistle as he saddled the horse, feeling the loneliness of the silent ranch yard settle on him.

Twenty minutes later, under the hottest midday sun, they were heading north toward the high band of red pines along the fence line. Except for the green needles, the expanse before him was featureless with silver, the shine of granite, and the flecked tips of sage leaves. They dipped down a steep bank covered with spiny grass into the creek bed. They'd always find the smart cattle there in the aspens, the cows that never lost their calves, that kept them close to their sides and away from the dangers, the dogs, the larkspur and water hemlock. Chief bolted at the first sight of the wide eyes from the trees, deep Hereford faces blazed with silver, and Hal reached forward to calm him with a touch under the mane.

They picked across the creek bed, still heading north, and lurched up the other side, now about two miles from the house and five hundred feet higher. The ground was bony with round rocks that kept giving Chief fits with a rasp of steel against stone. It was no land for horses or men. And what about his daughters, Sarah with her pink glasses and Louisa towing all her many friends like a train of open-mouthed cabooses— was this where they should be? If he had done what

Allen Fetchko called the right thing, what would have become of his girls? There were marks left by the kind of solitude children feel in the deep ranch winters, marks Hal could still find in the faces of the men at Peltzer's, or in the voices of the women unwrapping their dishes in the parish-house kitchen.

But Hal knew that this solitude was what had brought his father out to stay so many years ago. The summer he was seventeen he caught tuberculosis from his sister's French nurse, and his parents sent him out to a convalescent home in Arizona. It was 1935, still an age when Europeans hired surgeons and guides and spent the fall ranging the West for grizzlies and mountain goats. Frederick, as his parents called him, was a handsome boy, a little too thin, but he had already learned to use silence as a weapon. He ran away from the home and headed out for his own tour of the West. Hal had seen a picture of him then, posed in front of the Tetons, and the camera had caught something punishing in those wide-set eyes and broad, open smile.

Hal reached the pines, now about fifty-five hundred feet, and he dismounted to give Chief a blow. Hal checked his hooves and shoes, and ran his hand under the saddle blanket and loosened cinch. Far below he could see the ranch yard, and he could almost imagine the way it must have looked the day his father, finished with Yale now, brought Jean back with him after a tented wedding in Philadelphia. She told Hal she understood, from that day on, what the pioneer wives felt as they waited in the wagons, dreaming of the green hills of Ohio, while husbands made homes out of sod and buffalo skin.

When the war began, his father was a cattle rancher with two months' experience, and he won an occupational deferment much as Hal did with teaching thirty years later. Hal was not a good teacher, but his father contributed even less to the war effort in the form of food for the troops. Dead cattle and dying pastures forced him to the books, and made him realize he'd have to innovate to survive. So when his neighbors were buying one surplus Jeep apiece, he bought eight and mechanized everything, banishing draft horses forever from his sight. When others still believed the bovine species needed a free range to fatten right, Fred Shepley partitioned his thousand acres into a lattice of pastures, and rotated cattle with military precision into fallow fields that were as lush, relatively speaking, as Kentucky.

But there was no joy in it—Hal knew that now—for either his father or his mother. After three miscarriages, one of them during the terrifying hollowness of a Canadian blizzard that seemed to suck the fetus from her, she gave up on raising a family. But once more she got pregnant and carried this child to term and gave birth to Hal, and then, two years later, to Mark. She loved each of them more because the other was so different, as if, in her loneliness, she had created a whole circle of friends. When the skinny teenager Roy appeared at her door, as she was breaking

up a screaming fight between the boys, she let him in.
Maybe he was just one more to add to the circle, a
pretty band of misfits. Hal's father put him in the stacks
and left him there for good, even though, Hal remembered overhearing once, she asked him straight out
why he didn't give the boy a break.

Hal stood beside Chief and stared down at the layout
of a ranch yard he knew so well, pathways worn into
the grasses like lifelines on a palm. And then from
somewhere came the memory of a winter, of one winter night so cold the chickens' combs froze and broke
off and heifers died even as they stood side to side in
a protected shed. Hal awoke to the sound of wind and
of his mother's footsteps on the stairs. He kneeled on
his bed, scratched a peephole in the glass, and looked
out to see her working through the snow to the bunkhouse, where Roy must have been lying under every
blanket he could find. She would have found him
there, the fire cold, and Hal could picture her shaking
him awake, yelling at him to come into the house. And
he would have said, No, I'm fine. She must have said,
Don't be a fool, you'll die here. Hal might never know
what either of them said, but he did know what he saw
from the window, the two of them staggering back to
the house through the wind. In the morning, Hal found
him on the couch in the living room, and he looked
as if he planned to stand his ground and never leave.

When Hal mounted again, his legs were finally too
tired to fight the saddle, and he had his seat back.

Even if it was Mark who always won the rodeo events, Hal had the best seat. Coming to a crest into the low western sun he looked down a half mile and saw the yellow dirt of Easy Street. Chief longed for the road, the flat footing and the soft relief of warm sand. Hal let him pick his way on loose reins, and they dropped out onto the road just a few feet from the place where Roy, sober this time, had driven a Jeep into the ditch and broke his head open like a jar. He had spent five months in hospitals, first in Butte and later, when the doctors decided he needed a steel plate, in Boise. Hal had never before thought to ask this question, but who paid those medical bills?

Hal and Chief came to the last rise above the ranch. The sheds and barns were dark, and quiet, a peaceful scene with a few warm lights from the windows of the house. It was a strange way to make a living, though: breeding and weaning and feeding animals into food. Through it all, Hal's father had made sure the boys understood that point. He'd taken them to Iowa, to the plant, and the men made them wear hardhats that said "Milk is for cats," and "Beans make you fart." Hal watched the power wand touching the temple, and he heaved at the acrid smell of electrocution, at the sight of the endless belt of intestines and lungs. But whether the message was aimed at the cruelty of the younger boy or the kindness of the older, Hal never knew. And when his father died, it was in his bed in his J. Press pinpoint cotton pajamas, which, mailed to him annually, were the only luxury of his youth he'd never been able to lick.

Roy was seated at the head of the table, wearing a fresh orange shirt and a brand-new pair of blue jeans. It was six-thirty, a late meal for him, if Hal remembered the ranch schedule right, but he waited without complaint. Marcie was helping Jean at the "old stove." Hal sat at the other end, legs and groin burning and tightening from the ride. He glanced sideways at Marcie as she slid his plate in front of him and waited as his mother came quietly to the table.

"Well," said Jean, "how nice to be together."

Roy had already started to flick pieces of parsley out of his potatoes, but Marcie gave Jean an affirming smile. Hal heard this hopeful phrase—she always used to say things like that at special dinners, things like "How sad it would be to sit down with the family and not have fun," a wish for something better—and he knew that she had begun to relax. He'd now seen enough of them together to imagine them content, not talking much, but there had never been a lot of talk with his father either. He would have been ready to make his peace with the scene if only . . . it didn't seem like an end for *him*, a death of the family that Hal, alone, had cared about, but Mark, alone, had been able to preserve. So he started to imagine what Mark would do now, what kind of sly, slightly vulgar idea or comment would come from Mark to save everyone at the table from too much silence and too much regret. When the inspiration came he didn't stop to question or edit it, even to the point of mimicking Mark's constant mocking tone. He said, "This is a *celebration?* Let's go to the Four Aces and do it *right.*"

His mother finally said, "Why, Hal, I haven't been in that place in thirty years."

"No way and no thanks," said Marcie. She'd been there once with Hal before they were married.

Roy said nothing.

"Well, how 'bout it, Roy," said Hal, suddenly almost warming to the image of himself and Roy elbow to elbow.

"Been dry since '82, Hal."

An hour later he was sitting alone at the neon-lit bar of the Four Aces working through a mug of Olympia. The place smelled of spilled beer and toilet-bowl disinfectant, and the round wooden tables along the side wall of this narrow room were initialed and sticky. Above the beer signs and illuminated clocks hung a row of mounted trophies, including a large buck whose lower lip, long held firm by a packing of sawdust, was starting to droop. There were few people there, just a couple of young "professionals" deep into plans about reopening the silver mine, or buying the Mason Hotel building, or developing a motel on Route 80, and a joyless pickup under way between a salesman in a safari jacket and a girl in a T-shirt.

He moved out of earshot to a table in the corner. In the back, past the jukebox, he could see the bright light and hear the glassine crack of the pool table and balls. One summer he'd become a better than good pool shooter on that table; he hadn't held a cue in years. He sipped on his beer until the whole thing, the evening, the trip back to Millersburg, began to seem not just pointless but dangerous, a mistake that shuts out memory and changes a life for good. He decided to switch to Jack Daniel's, and as soon as the girl left him his first shot, the door opened and in walked Roy.

On the shock of the first sight, Hal thrilled at the idea of catching Roy, the real Roy, as Hal had known him all along. There were some murmurs and chuckles from the crowd, which had begun to grow into the evening. He watched Roy scan the room, but it wasn't the dry forced look of a drunk scouting out a good time, and suddenly Hal realized Roy had come for *him*. He stood up as Roy's eyes found him out, and waved him over.

"I'd like to sit if I could," said Roy.

"Sure. Of course."

Roy eased himself into a chair and took a few moments to decide what to do with his hands. They came to rest, palms down, side by side on the table. "Your mom asked me to come," he explained.

Hal could feel almost nothing but sympathy for this guileless man sent here against his will, but he had no words to offer.

"You know I got no secrets from you. Your mom asked me to stay and get married, and I did it."

Hal answered that he had no secrets either, and

even as he mouthed these empty words he realized they were true.

"I got no secrets about my life or where I been. I've made more mistakes than a flock of sheep."

To anyone else, Hal would have agreed he'd made his share too.

"I started drinking when I was fifteen. I've been in jail twice. Once for stealing a car—"

"You don't have to tell me all this."

"—and once for being incorrigibly vagrant. And that tells it." With this statement, Roy removed his hands from the table and leaned back. The young waitress came over and Roy showed her a slow, almost fatherly smile, and ordered a Coke for himself and another bourbon for Hal.

He started up again in his jumpy sentences, and told Hal that many times over the years Hal's father had given up on him, tried to fire him and break him out for good. It was Jean who got him his job back. She had saved him more than once, one night chasing him to Butte when he figured he was just hitchhiking to a place to die. And when his life finally brushed the roof of hell—he was in California then—it was Jean, the better memories of those bitter years, that made him quit drinking. It had been easy enough to catch the wagon; after a lifetime the drinker in him had become a separate being that left without a trace. But it took him five years, working as a janitor and dishwasher in a motel in Stockton, to decide to go back to Millersburg to see her one last time. "I just wanted to tell her thanks. And I wanted her to remember me."

"Did you know Dad was dead?"

He didn't answer Hal's question. "I never really knew your dad. No one did. But this was sure: nothing came natural to the man. Nothing at all." It sure wasn't ranching, Roy went on, though he'd become one of the best ranchers in Montana. And it sure wasn't raising a family.

"I'll give it to you straight," said Roy. "I hated the man. And there's one thing I'll never forgive his memory for. It was the way he looked at his family and saw right through them, right out the other side, as if they was nothing to take pride in."

"Good God," said Hal. "You knew that?"

"Just because I was drunk didn't mean I was deaf. I used to watch you and Markie fighting over who would sit next to him in the pickup. I coulda told you to forget it. It made me sad, seeing you kids try to please him."

"But you just looked the other way."

"Well, maybe that's the way it seems now. But I recall I taught Markie to drive and, Hal, I like to think I was your friend too."

"But, Roy—"

"Oh sure," Roy said quickly, "it may sound a little strange now, and there's no forgetting, but I like to think what Jean favored in me when there was so much not to is the feelings I had for you boys."

"That isn't what I—"

Roy pushed forward. "When Jean asked me to marry her, the first question in my mind was would you boys allow it? And now it's done. We all got plenty to get used to, but I like to hope the good I tried to do in the past makes up for the bad I couldn't help."

Hal asked Roy if he was finished. Roy nodded, and then sat back, comfortable at last.

"You want to know what *I* remember. I remember you teaching Mark how to drive. I remember you taught Mark all those knots." His voice was fast and hard. "I remember all those evenings you and Mark sat in the equipment shed. You never did anything for me," he shouted. "It was Mark. Always Markie."

Hal wanted to go on—he could picture hundreds of times he'd watched Roy and Mark head off together in the Jeep—but none of it was having the effect he wanted. He wanted Roy to apologize, and when Roy did, Hal would forgive him, perhaps even really forgive him. But the more he tried to heap on Roy, the more Roy sat quietly protected in a kind of wisdom, a patience that bored into Hal like a spruce worm. And when Roy finally responded, it was quiet, and low, and kind.

"You weren't wanting to learn things from me. You was still holding out for your dad."

"No. No."

"You was too. You needed something different than Mark. You needed a harder thing."

"I didn't expect anything from you. I never did."

"I used to try. You wanted to know why the bulls

never recognized their calves. You wanted to know what would happen if gravity let go. You asked me why the other fellas laughed at me. Can you figure a fella like me, sick with drink, answering questions like that?"

"Those were just *kid's* questions," he snapped back. "They don't need answers that make *sense.*"

"I'll tell you the truth, Hal. You scared me to death."

Hal was sitting forward, leaning way over the table. He noticed for the first time that people in the darkness behind Roy were watching them. But already stirring in Hal was something beyond hurt, the picture of a ten-year-old with a T-shirt too loose at the neck and an oversize belt, and he saw in front of the boy a sick, frightened man with no place to go, a man who had nothing but could still, somehow, lose everything. Hal could taste the loneliness in the boy and the man like the sharp hit of tinfoil in the mouth.

"I thought you just didn't like me," Hal said.

"I tried to be there if you wanted me."

Hal said nothing for a few minutes. The bar was full now; the bargirl had been called every nickname; smoke from a hundred cigarettes, lit all at once, lowered the ceiling above like a killing frost. Roy sat unruffled: the patience, the wisdom.

"At least you weren't born into this screwy family," Hal said finally.

"I guess not, Hal, but it was always something more than day wages."

* * *

He awoke to the sound of laughter. It was Marcie's high-pitched laugh, breaking into the air, dying, breaking again even louder. He looked out the window to see the white haze of mid-morning sun. His head throbbed, because after Roy left the Four Aces he had stayed to finish his bourbon, and a few faces he barely recalled asked him if he still played pool. Some things a town never forgets. He had switched to tequila, because that was what they were playing for, and in the end he wasn't so much staggering as walking in bursts.

He crawled out of bed and began stepping down the hall to the bathroom. He heard more laughing from Marcie—he figured now she was on the veranda—and he ducked into his old room to take up again, after all these years, his vantage post at the window above the chaise.

First he saw his mother, her shirttails flapping, off in the corner of her garden digging up her precious bulbs to save them from the merciless Montana winter. She wore a bright yellow bandanna and green work gloves, and she stopped for a moment to straighten her back and glance back at the others. He followed her gaze and saw Marcie, wearing her running suit, stretched on the chaise, thin and fit down her long thighs and to her narrow ankles. Roy was sitting next to her, leaning forward so he could practically whisper in her ear. Between them was a small redwood table with coffee cups and the remains of a coffee cake.

Roy's story was now coming to an end. Marcie suddenly became so convulsed that she leaned back with her legs drawn up. She looked to Hal like their daughters, Louisa and Sarah. When she was done, both of them sat still, and Jean straightened again, and the three of them looked out at the high passes of the freshly whitened mountains. There was a slight breeze that made the grasses float all the way to the pines.

Roy stood up, hiking his pants over his bony hips and looking so very old. He walked around behind Marcie's chaise in a slow, almost courtly manner. Then, while Hal spied on them in amazement, old Roy, the old drunk that his father had once literally and bodily thrown out of the second-story hayloft, this same Roy bent down to give his wife a light, dancing kiss on the top of the head. Hal reached his hand to the top of his own head, and touched the spot Roy had kissed. And it was then, for the first time, that Hal realized he didn't know, had never known, the last name of the man who was now his mother's husband.

Norfolk, 1969

_____

HE REMEMBERS THE HEAT, the first summer in Norfolk, the summer of '69. He remembers the way it felt as it radiated from the steel decks, rising so fast that it pulled the breath out of his lungs. He remembers bringing it home on his uniform like the smells of paint and fuel oil. He remembers watching the withering lindens on the median strip of Military Boulevard as they struggled for life and air. He remembers those days at Virginia Beach, when the heat pushed them to the edge of the sea like a ribbon of survivors running from the flames.

And he remembers the day they arrived, young, frightened, as if the possibility of going to war was nothing compared to the certainty of calling this place home. They were lost on those miracle miles and plastic strips, returning helplessly again and again to an immense Pontiac dealership floating on a sea of asphalt. They drove past shopping centers, garden-apartment complexes, bungalows with brown lawns, all of them locked tight against the hot air. They did not need to ask each other, How will we survive here? They were sure they would not. Each time they completed a fruitless circle he could feel the accusation rise: This, out of all the alternatives, this is the choice *you* made. This is Norfolk.

They drove in silence, no longer entirely sure of what they were looking for. They kept believing one of those strips of tar and concrete would lead to a downtown, something familiar, like a white meetinghouse with maples and elms, or a cityscape with seafood restaurants along the waterfront. They'd planned to stop there first, kept thinking on the long, barren drive down to the tip of Cape Charles that there would still be this buffer, this nice lunch alone. But there was no center. The city of Norfolk seemed less the reason for these traffic islands and power lines than the result of them. Finally they ran out of time and asked a man where the Navy base was, and he laughed and made a 360-degree gesture. She cried, and when he, in his alien white uniform soaked with sweat, reached over to comfort her—she cannot have forgotten this—she ripped off his shoulder board and threw it into the back seat. He panicked: how could he, an ensign of two weeks, report to his first ship with a sleeve ripped to the armpit? Then they both cried.

They cried again, four months later, gripping each other in bed the morning the ship left Norfolk. Six, seven months apart—the thought had been catching them both at odd moments for weeks, a slow suffocation. Soon they were making plans for weekends and then realizing the date fell into a dark hole. They looked forward in time like mapmakers writing Here There Be Dragons at the edge of the earth. Maybe they can be faulted now for their terrors. His ship wasn't a man-of-war; it was a floating refrigerator, a spare-parts bin that made deliveries. He wasn't going to Vietnam, wasn't even going to the seas off Vietnam, but to the Mediterranean, to Naples, Barcelona, Athens, and Tangier. Physically he would be in no danger, but there were dragons awaiting just the same.

The U.S.S. *Jupiter* departed Norfolk on the first of October, just after the heat of that long summer broke for good. When the tugs came alongside and the last line was cast off the pier, and when, in turn, the tugs cast off and the *Jupiter* worked her way down Hampton Roads and through the narrow breaks of the Chesapeake Bay Bridge-Tunnel and out finally to sea, Ensign Charles A. Martin, USNR, stood at his appointed Sea and Anchor watch on the fantail and thought about Julie. Boo-hoo, the executive officer had said to him when he walked aboard after a last kiss on the dock. It was meant kindly. He said, Sailors find other pleasures. But you chose this, Charlie wanted to say. It's your career. He watched the froth of the screw etching out a slender line to home until somewhere it began to break and was finally reclaimed by a smooth surface, without consequence or change.

During the first few days, the sea and the shipboard world of order and purpose infused the career men with an almost childlike energy. The cruise, the chance for adventure and career enhancements, rough seas and sheltered ports—this was what occupied their private thoughts. In small miserable groups, Charlie Martin and his friends tried to ridicule the spluttering excitement the lifers could not conceal. Did you see the captain when we cast off the last line? said one. He had an *orgasm.* How Charlie wanted his superiors to know he hated this voyage. On land he might have been able to hurt them, the way scenes of protest and rebellion on the nightly news bore into their hearts, lodged well under their skin. But here now, under way at sea, the sailors were free.

During those months, awaking to men in khakis and dungarees, passing hours in steel rooms, closing out days at vigilant watches on the black seas, he grieved for her. At midnight, in the hushed chatter of the bridge lit with red bulbs and radar screens, lulled by a gentle swell and the vibrating pulse of the propeller shaft, five hundred men asleep under his feet, during this most private time he gave everything to her. He recalled her in every mood and in every place, everything they had shared. During slow watches, he kept awake by reconstructing the events of their first ten dates—what they said, what she wore.

As perfect as his memory was for these details, they were not enough to keep her whole in his mind. Two months out, three months, she began to break up under the swells; she became foreign, a vision no longer completely believable. How strange it seemed that in this world were people with soft cheeks and slender waists, people who wore clothes printed with lavender flowers and dancing cats. Sex one never forgets, but the loveliness of hair and the delicacy of wrists, these fade like photographs left in the sun. When he read her letters they gave him joy, but it was her girlish script that fascinated him—concrete proof that a civilization, now lost, had once covered the earth. So he read her letters thinking more of the female hand that wrote them than the news, the details, the inner thoughts. And if, at that, he missed something, a cry for help or the beginning of a loss of heart, perhaps it can be forgiven now.

Maybe he should have kept his memories alive with the whores who waited every time he stepped on dry land. The first time they came into Naples, passing through Ischia and Capri on the way toward the dark shape of Vesuvius hidden in yellow, acrid clouds, Charlie knew what to expect. At the pier there were lines of them, ready in white boots and leather minis, as if the U.S. Navy had called them all at home and told them to expect the *Jupiter* at three. As the men stepped out of the launch in a line, they were joined one by one by a partner, like bridesmaids and ushers walking up the aisle. In the bars and nightclubs the girls were more circumspect, waiting while the sailors finished the first drink, waiting until they'd widened the circle to permit one more chair, and then another, until at last each man had turned to an attentive, familiar face at his side. At midnight the Campfire Girls came out into the streets, gathered in small clumps at each corner, lit and warmed by bonfires burning on the sidewalk; in the early morning the piles of ash remained like broken camps on a battlefield, and then the water truck came by and hosed the residue of lost nights into the gutter.

Several times the helicopter pilots invented reasons to fly to Rome for an overnight, and the XO indulgently looked the other way while Charlie and a couple of friends hooked a ride. They took a *pensione* room together just like on ship, showering and dressing like high-schoolers, and then went out to tour the Forum, eat overlooking the Tiber, and finish the evening drinking beer at a sidewalk café on the Via Veneto. They would pretend to be conversing until one of those elegant, cosmopolitan women—no whores here, they thought—might happen to glance their way and the three of them would stiffen, wondering, Does she know I am alive and full of need? Even then Charlie knew they were pathetic; even then he understood that three young seminarians would have gotten into more mischief than they did, young and free, with pockets full of money, separated from vows.

One time the *Jupiter* stayed out at sea for fifty-six days. That was the time they left for Barcelona and ended up off the coast of Lebanon. There was a crisis on; the *Kennedy* left Norfolk with no warning at all and picked up a ragtag task force coming through

Gibraltar, and the *Jupiter* was the only fast supply ship on station to greet them. There may have been some danger, but no one in the *Jupiter* would have noticed if an errant Israeli missile had taken off the stack. Every morning at first light the *Jupiter* took its lumbering place in the center of the formation and the warships came alongside hour after hour for frozen meat and spare parts, for movies and mail. During the night, inside the steel and aluminum shell darkened to war-time conditions, the lights blazed; through the night the crew opened the holds and refrigerators and pre-pared the orders for the next day. In the wardroom, given over to cafeteria style against all tradition, Char-lie and his fellow reserve officers looked at each other stupefied, each face wondering how it was, just how it had turned out that they were there at all, so tired, working so hard at a job they could barely understand. Charlie hoped against hope when the engineers said, If number-two evaporator craps out, we'll have to go back to Norfolk. It never did. He listened eagerly as the supply officers said, It won't be long now—the holds are almost empty. And then one morning, stand-ing off in the mist of dawn, Charlie saw not another destroyer or LSD but the *Jupiter*'s sister ship, the *Sylvania*, loaded in Norfolk and crewed by men who really didn't mind a quick four-week trip to the Mediterra-nean in the middle of winter, as long as it meant the *Jupiter* would have to stay on for another four months. How jaunty the *Sylvania*'s officers sounded on the radio-telephone as the ships steamed alongside, tethered by lines fore and aft, the *Jupiter*'s holds filling once again. When the men of the *Sylvania* unfolded their banner saying *We deliver* and played "Carry Me Back to Old Virginny" on their topside loudspeakers as they finally sailed away at the end of the day, even the captain swore at them. That's how tired they were. And the next morning at five-thirty the *Jupiter* waited low in the water as the destroyers and LSDs began their approach.

So it was fifty-six days before they came back to their old Italian home, and there, as always, the whores waited. The one that landed by Charlie's side was new and didn't know not to bother. After the past two months it did not surprise him that she seemed prettier, sweeter, than any other ever had to him, that he indeed might have found the one whore in Naples that some sailor should have taken home to Iowa, ring on finger. Together they walked up to the Galleria, and she asked him to buy her a gin and he did. The waiter brought her water and charged him four thousand lire, and he drank coffee and smoked cigarettes, and she waved her hands in the direction of Pozzuoli and pointed to herself, smiling, saying *Mia casa*, and he said, New Hampshire, and pointed to himself. At that moment he would have filled her purse with lire, Marlboros, Rolex watches, if she had consented to buy a nightgown and come with him to the Ambassador, let him watch her comb her hair, and then crawl in beside him to fall asleep. He would have slept for twenty hours, and she hardly could have minded. But when at last she said, Fun? to him, he was too slow, and she went off angrily, not even trying to be discreet when the waiter handed her a thousand-lire bill.

Whether Julie wanted it or not, when the *Jupiter* finally turned for home after eight months, Charlie was unspoiled. They passed through Gibraltar at night, and the next morning, out of sight of land, the work on the ship stopped. They shuffled some papers and stood their watches, but there was no need for deception; this crew had worked as hard as the Navy could work it, and now they were going home. The engineers and supply types, whose normal places of duty were the engine rooms and holds, came up on deck and the officers came up to the bridge and clustered around the chart table, studying those arcane scribbles with unusual interest. The visitors stood on the wings of the bridge for hours, staring west, freely distracting the watch from the normal prescribed routine. Without much danger of running into anything a thousand miles at sea, Charlie and his friends could relax. A year ago they had been college boys who knew nothing of the sea and now they had seen every hazard the Mediterranean could offer, the merchantmen on automatic pilot, the fleets of fishing boats, the shoals and straits. They had passed late nights terrified of collisions and had calculated nervously the distance it would take to stop the ship at All Back Emergency should it ever be necessary. And now, with the cruise almost done, they could thrill at the forward momentum of this huge mass toward home, as if they no longer had anything to fear even if the *Jupiter* plowed straight through Hampton Roads and came to a stop somewhere west of Richmond.

But a slack attitude and an end of fear were not the only changes that Charlie noticed on this crossing west. A day out of Gibraltar something began to happen to the *Jupiter*, as if all the steel and electronics and weapons were façade, an illusion that had concealed a primitive open boat at the heart. By the first evening she had left behind the dying ocher waters of the Mediterranean and was surrounded by clear seas full of life. Five hundred miles out, Charlie saw seven or eight Cory's shearwaters sailing stiff-winged at the wave tops, crossing the bow and proceeding toward some indistinguishable watery landmark. Charlie could barely understand what was happening, but suddenly he looked from side to side and found himself flying with these birds, sharing the sea and air. The farther the *Jupiter* plowed toward the center of the ocean, the more an elemental soul asserted itself, swells of time, growing over a million square miles. Each day they sailed deeper into the past, where radars went blank and lorans went silent, and slack days with shimmering sea piled on gray days with black waves. In the middle of the ocean Charlie sighted the funnel of a ship at the horizon, and its smoke, ugly and brown at the source, looked in the sun like gray-white sails, and he suddenly understood why whaling ships used to log "Ships Spoken" with a tone almost of rejoicing. The captain ordered a course change to come closer, and

Charlie dipped the ensign in response to a smart salute from such a tired steamer. Both ships stopped engines and the two ships rose and fell in tune, and in harmony with the sea. The two crews lined the rails, staring and waving. The signalmen, volubly conversing in a language all their own, clacked off messages with their lamps, and brought down to the bridge a greeting from a Libyan captain that said, Wish of good weather to American Navy.

So perhaps it wasn't so curious that this same Navy that had seemed to be the cause of such pain to Charlie also gave him the most sustained period of joy he had ever experienced. For it was during those ten days that a bursting lump of ecstasy settled in his chest and kept him breathless. It was Julie, he told himself again and again, the return to Julie, so loved and missed, that was now opening his heart to spirits he'd never imagined. But he was not telling himself the truth, just as he did not tell her the truth when finally they were together again. Because Charlie had fallen in love, given an unfamiliar pledge, an unspoken vow to this voyage almost done, and—how he would have resisted this eight months ago—to this ship. It was as if everywhere he went, from the signal bridge to the bilge, he found parts of himself, pieces of brass polished and smoothed by his own hand, as if he were blind but had sight in such well-known space. None of the anguishes of the age, none of the compromises that had been forced upon him, none of the political confusions in his head, mattered anymore.

How clearly he remembers the day they returned to Norfolk. The watch sighted Chesapeake Light a little before six, in the mist, so perfect in time and place that it seemed a ghostly product of the navigator's black arts. As the sun rose a stormy petrel found them, looking more like a barn swallow than a seabird as it perched on a voice tube and crapped quietly on the deck. Charlie had the watch that morning, but the bridge was cramped with sightseers; the night before, the radiomen picked up the first commercial AM station and the XO piped it all over the ship. The sounds were full of unfamiliar names, groups that had come up from nowhere while Charlie listened to European remakes of the hits of the fifties. Through the night Charlie listened to that station with something—how could there have been room for such rival energies—like sadness, even as the thought of Julie welcoming him home only hours from now made him cry with relief.

He had no trouble spotting her on the pier; he didn't need a turn with the binoculars being passed from hand to hand. There was a dense crowd of women and children. It was the variety of colors that struck him first, the screaming pinks and purples, violent yellows. After the somber dress of the European women the gathering could well have been mistaken for a troupe of clowns. Fat wives in pantsuits held up infants with American flags taped to their wrists; a large family displayed a long banner saying Welcome Home, Daddy. Several of the chiefs' wives, veterans of the event, had brought aluminum lawn chairs and had taken their privileged places in a line at the front. The captain's wife waited in her Buick at the head of the pier. There was a band in place as well, an unexpected note of festivity for everyone, a rarity for a mere supply ship, but provided out of respect for a cruise that ran well over the six-month limit.

Julie was standing apart from all this, disgusted— how clearly he could read it on her face even when her head was a small dot in the crowd—with the circus and determined to keep this moment private. He loved her for that, even as he wished, for this one moment, that she could forget how she hated the Navy, that she could welcome him back as the Sailor's Wife, that strange and precious creature he had created and had been living with throughout the cruise. He knew that there was joy behind her look, that the sullenness of her wave was not for him, but as the other officers on the bridge—all of them suddenly equal—pointed out their shipmates' wives and families, they were silent about her.

They were nervous when they met. She sat in his office preoccupied as he signed the last leave papers for his men. There was a strange echo in their voices as they drove home, a hollowness to the mundane chatter that, after so long, seemed outdone by the waiting. He gave her presents—Spanish leather, French perfume, a folding chair of Italian design— with the feeling that he might have been thinking of someone else when he selected them. And their first lovemaking was tentative, as if they were afraid of finding changes or the fingerprints of others. But they both knew that these first few hours could not be otherwise, and in the evening, after they had settled onto their tiny square of lawn, with the sun setting over the gas station next door, the quick answers began to lengthen into longer stories. They began to reclaim bits of their time apart, and they were happy.

The voyage done, Charlie resumed his episodic life in Norfolk. The ship went into dry dock a week after they returned, and with the exception of regular nights on duty, he worked the orderly hours of a businessman. He had plans stretching out for weeks with no fear of week-long training cruises or unscheduled runs to the Caribbean. Together they spent evenings at the Giant, a hangar-like market where they bought steaks in the meat department and took them to be cooked in the barbecue department; they cut lines in five-screen movie houses, spending six or seven hours inside on a single ticket. These were modest pleasures, but they represented a normal domestic life—or, at least, the continuation of a normal college life—and Charlie pursued them with all his heart. They passed an afternoon working up a strip of car dealerships posing as shoppers, selecting air-conditioned Cadillacs, Bonnevilles, and Lincolns for test drives. They returned to Virginia Beach with his shipboard friends in the kind of large boisterous groups that leave solitary bathers feeling lonely and unnoticed. They went to performances of the Norfolk Symphony, which began each concert with the National Anthem, everyone bellowing like baseball fans.

This was Charlie's Norfolk, the one he had left behind eight months ago, the one they had discovered whole the first day they drove in. At first, there was nothing to make him think that Julie had discovered anything different. But she had taken to drinking herbal tea while he'd been gone, and she had two or three varieties in the cupboard that certainly weren't offered by the Giant. And she'd bought a pair of boots with studded patterns that she'd found, she said, in a place across town. And then, one night, she announced that a folksinger she liked was playing in a coffeehouse near the museum, and why didn't they go? A coffeehouse? In Norfolk? He could not imagine that such a thing existed, and was still stunned as they threaded through a darkened room of small round tables to the tunes of Dylan and the Weavers. He wondered why she hadn't taken him there sooner, even the night he landed.

But as they sat, something unexpected began to grow inside him. When his eyes adjusted to the light he saw long hair, bell-bottoms, and beads. He should have felt he was among his own kind, but did not. The protest songs—songs he knew well—seemed simplistic, and the knowing laughter from the crowd had a smugness he no longer thought was earned. He began to feel cramped at this corner table, and he had the sudden vision that he was being stared at, which might well have been true, because Navy men were unmistakable in Norfolk. He felt as if the audience was taking his measure and finding him unsatisfactory. Julie looked at him nervously—she knew instantly that something was wrong—asking if he wanted to leave, apologizing each time the waitress slammed into his chair. No, he said. It's fabulous. How did you ever find it? But when they finally stepped out into the night air his relief was overwhelming.

In the days and weeks that followed she unfolded to him the rest of the Norfolk she had been living in since he'd left. She showed him a bedraggled, secluded Victorian neighborhood that felt like a village around whose walls a city had grown; there were God's Eyes and Sister Corita banners in window after window, and music from loudspeakers fighting house-to-house; the streets were lined with old Volvos and half-disassembled VW minibuses. They shopped at a unisex boutique run by a transvestite named Irving, who clothed him in bell-bottoms, tie-dyed shirts, and fringed leather vests which today, appearing in foot-lockers and cardboard boxes, make him laugh out loud. She showed him a community scattered across the city, head shops brazenly nestled between Safe-ways and 7-Eleven stores. And Julie, like a conductor on the underground railroad, knew every stop.

One by one—a chance meeting on Mowbray Arch, beers after an opening at the museum—a whole new group came into his life, and by degrees Charlie began to understand his Julie and the time she had spent alone. It had surprised him, during the first few weeks when they gathered with Navy friends, to hear the women referring to her, slightly hurt and peevish, as a stranger. Charlie had developed a very lonely picture of her solitary life, returning home after work to the apartment, cooking something simple, playing records. The fact was that this picture was accurate but not complete. There had been no lack of people in her life. They were artists and Old Dominion University faculty members, newspaper reporters working on novels, hippies plotting disruptions at the Navy base, black sheep from old Virginia families, a few pleasant but confused souls who didn't know what they were. They lived in the attic apartments along the Arch or in feminist communities in Chesapeake. They gave parties in studios and warehouses, smoked marijuana, and made veiled references to LSD trips.

If anything about himself during those days had been relaxed or sure, he would have embraced these people. Perhaps if they had been warmer to him, his life might have turned out differently. Julie denied it angrily, but his return from the Mediterranean was an irritation to them and his presence was tolerated only because of her. She was the star for them; he was a previously undiscovered and cold asteroid that occasionally dimmed her light. They were kind enough in general gatherings, but when the talk turned serious they saved everything for her and revealed nothing in his presence. Half the time he spent with them it seemed someone was whispering in someone's ear, or sharing knowing looks, or disappearing into the kitchen for a muffled conversation. He could gain a passing audience when he, a Navy officer, harangued most vehemently against the war or when he disdainfully passed along military secrets. They'd listen, congratulate him on his wisdom, and then patronize him into nothingness. Julie saw him struggling to be liked and to like, and she tried to help. But, as much as she tried, she never quite overcame a conviction in his heart that she agreed with her friends that, in these temples of the sixties, her husband, Charlie, was unwashed.

At least, that was how it looked to him. He understood only too well how they threatened him and how he resisted her new life. But one night with the group, toward the end of summer, ended any deception. As they sat down to after-dinner marijuana, the conversation shifted to a backpacking trip someone was planning in the Shenandoah, and they talked for a time about quiet communion with nature. Charlie said that actually that was something he had experienced rather strongly at sea. He talked of the endless swells and the storms, the play of porpoises, the seabirds he had learned to identify. He tried to describe the sensation of being lifted into flight with the shearwaters. He talked about the fraternity of running lights in the dark, ships passing in the unquestioned knowledge that here, on the ocean, man and his ships were not intruders but subjects accepted and ruled by natural law.

He knew he had gotten carried away: it was the first time since he'd met them that he really believed he had something to share on an equal footing. As he finished, eyes misting with awe, he recognized that he might have bored the group with these sea stories. But it was not boredom he saw when he glanced around the room. Somewhere in his ramblings he had sailed quite irretrievably out into politics. He felt the room turn to bone. He looked quickly at Julie, who had heard all of this before, and she was scarlet with embarrassment, dumb with surprise. What had he said? He suddenly had no memory of what he had been talking about. How had he offended so completely? Well, said someone at length into the silence, there is now time for an opposing view.

And then, humiliated, feeling alone and misunderstood, Charlie lost his temper. An opposing view? he asked. Opposing what? Just what had he said that would offend their delicate political sensibilities? Teach me, he said sneeringly. He went on, attacking with full machete swings, accusing them of being simplistic, fascistic, superficial, and middle class.

After she had bundled him out of there—with a few obligatory words all around about the positive value of disagreement—and after his anger had turned to hurt and despair, she told him everything. They sat on their bed, beside a large silver-framed wedding portrait, and she said she had wanted to die during the first months of separation. She said she had hated him for abandoning her in Norfolk. She said each time she addressed letters to the ship, and each time she received his from the ship, the word *Jupiter* made her retch. And then, she said, she had decided to survive, and she had found these friends far away from the Navy and they were good to her. She said that when it was all said and done, his ship had come back too soon, that she was just beginning to find herself, the self that had been buried by him, by their young marriage, by the Navy. And she said that she had not been unfaithful to him, physically, but she had wanted to, often and desperately, and she wished that he had been unfaithful to her.

The next night Charlie stood on the quarterdeck of the ship and resolved to save this marriage. He would save this love by degrees, by talk, by honesty, by giving freedom to her where he could, and taking it from her where he dared. But there was a cloud hanging over these resolutions, darker and darker as September came and went. The throng of yard workers, which in the early summer had dismantled the guts of the ship, had been for some time reassembling the pieces, and what had once been so reassuringly immobile and helpless was becoming once again a vessel fit for the high seas. The crew, which had been allowed to shrink through discharges and transfers, was now growing to full complement, and daily he saw new faces in his division. The talk among the career officers, for months concerned with repair orders and training, had turned to ops plans and port calls. All that remained was a few week-long shakedowns, and a firm date for the final departure. When it came—December 5—it was as if the line he had been paying out had come, at last, to the bitter end. They both wept the night he brought home that news, holding on to each other as they had the last time, older now but still frightened. It was not love they had lost; it was not that anger had replaced sadness. But this time they understood how little they could change.

And it was also true that Julie was, just then, in the midst of organizing a Norfolk contingent for the March on Washington, and had her hands full every evening with phone calls, buses to charter, box lunches, negotiation among factions. It was the kind of thing she did so very well. She had taken on this responsibility without consulting Charlie and had made no real effort to ask his thoughts on any of the issues. But he believed the war had to stop—he believed it as strongly as she did—and had decided weeks earlier that in this demonstration there was a place for him, a place big enough to encompass the paradoxes and complexities of his life in Norfolk. With his enthusiasm for the event his stock rose among her friends; they even thought of him as a bit of a catch, even though he refused to risk wearing his uniform on the march. Their apartment became a drop-in center for the people involved, hippies, Navy sons and daughters, young officers, and not a few enlisted men who winked and gave him the peace sign when they discovered what he was.

They left for Washington in a caravan of buses at five in the morning on that November 15, banners and slogans taped to the sides, American and North Vietnamese flags stuck out the windows. Charlie sat beside Julie in the privileged front seat of the lead bus. They navigated the crowd on the Mall as a group, and found room at the rally about halfway between the stage and the monument. Charlie could have predicted every word of every speech, but he was entranced, held silent by the gentle offering of a quartet from the Cleveland Symphony Orchestra; he hooted at the unexpected appearance of Earl Scruggs; he was overloaded by the entire cast of *Hair*, who, at the moment they sang "Let the Sunshine In," released hundreds of white doves, one of which landed next to their group and was patted and kissed until its tail feathers began to fall out. No one could have been unmoved, and Charlie would have been happy to end it at that point, to walk back to the buses arm in arm with Julie, with the private feeling that he had triumphed, at long last, over the fears in his heart and had won, finally, a place in his time.

But Julie was not ready for it to end, nor were many of the others in the group, and they made plans to join the smaller, unauthorized assault on the Justice Department. He knew there would be trouble, as indeed there was. He said he could not risk being arrested, the Navy could really come down on him, and his excuse was quickly accepted. What would have happened if she had argued with him, persuaded him to come along? Could she, even today, understand how desperately one part of him wanted to go with her? But there was no time or peace to understand these things; he asked her to be careful and said he would hold two buses for an hour.

Charlie stood in his place under the monument and watched the band head off for new conquests. Where only minutes before there had been four hundred thousand people, there was now a handful, some folding blankets, some hunting for lost bracelets and glasses in the battered grass. There were several doves on the ground, frightened to death by the unwilling part they had played in this pageant. A couple was trying to comfort or treat or revive a terrified teenager with a head full of drugs and a dark spot on her jeans where she had wet her pants. Up higher on the hill a fight had broken out, and all over Washington the gray sky closed down toward night.

And now, when he looks back on the sixties, this is where Charlie Martin remembers himself, standing on that discarded spot, held by something in him from birth, or something remaining from that joyful crossing home six months earlier. When he came back from the next cruise Julie was not on the pier; she had left Norfolk, and him, by then. When his three years were up, he thought fleetingly, but hard, about staying in for three more, but there was never any chance that he would make a career in the Navy, just as there was never any chance that he would throw rocks and balloons full of pig blood at the Justice Department walls.

The time for such choices was soon past, and the middle of the road widened enough for Charlie to leave behind the painful discoveries of youth and first love. What remained of Julie, and Norfolk, and the sixties, was the sea, boundless and inexhaustible, the mystery and the source.

Hole in the Day

SIX HOURS AGO Lonnie took one last look at Grant, at the oily flowered curtains and the kerosene heater, the tangled bed and the chipped white stove, at the very light of the place that was dim no matter how bright and was unlike any light she'd ever known before, and she ran. She ran from that single weathered dot on the plains because the babies that kept coming out of her were not going to stop, a new one was just beginning and she could already feel the suckling at her breast. Soon she will cross into Montana, or Minnesota, or Nebraska; she's just driving and it doesn't really matter to her where, because she is never coming back.

Grant sits in the darkened parlor room, still and silent. He's only twenty-nine, but he's got four children. It's five-thirty, maybe six in the morning. He's in his Jockeys, and his long legs and arms are brushed with the white of his blond hair. He feels as if the roof of his house has been lifted, as if he's being stalked by a drafting eagle high above. Straight ahead of him on the other wall, above the sofa and framed in weathered board, is a picture of mountains, of Glacier Park, but Grant isn't looking at the picture, it was Lonnie's. He is listening to the sound of the grass, a hum of voices, millions of souls, like locusts. Outside, there is a purple dawn over the yellow land, reaching toward this single house, and a clothesline pole standing outside casts a long, heaving shadow. There is a worn lawn between the house and garage, and beyond that in the rise and fall of Haakon County there is nothing, but still always something, maybe it's just a pheasant or a pronghorn, or maybe it's something you don't want to stare hard enough to find, like swimming in the river and looking straight down into the deep.

Grant shifts his weight off the thigh that's fallen asleep on the wooden edge of his sagging easy chair. He's got his twenty-gauge bird gun at his side, but it isn't loaded, it's just there. The grass tells him to forget her, *Forget Lonnie the whore.* There is a sigh from the kids' bedroom, a sigh and a rustle. Through the half-opened door of his bedroom Grant can see the tangled sheets where she stopped him last night a few inches away, left him hunched over an erection dying in its rubber sheath, a precaution taken too late and too sporadically to save her. The white dresser on the far side is now empty, the small bottles and pink boxes swept off the top into a duffel bag that she shut with a loud snap from the clasp. Grant had watched from the chair, and his mouth had settled open. *Lonnie the whore*, sings the grass, and Grant cannot resist the song, even though he knows she's never been unfaithful.

The kids' door opens and five-year-old Scott comes out, sees Grant, comes over, and stands at his father's side for a minute or two until he understands there will be no response. He goes off to the kitchen, hoping to find his mother, and does not come back. Grant hears the rest of them stirring, but he cannot help them, he's not sitting there. He's out on the plains, swooping low over a pack of coy dogs, looking for the bitch Lonnie; he's up on the light brown waters of the Cheyenne, waist-deep and getting ready to launch out naked into the passing root clumps and cedar hulks. He's standing on a four corners in the middle of the grass, underneath the solid dome of silver sky, and he feels the hills dark in the west, and he knows that is where she's headed.

Grant looks at Leila, his oldest; she's eight, sandy and freckled, already almost as tall as her mother. Grant understands that she has been talking to him, remembers that she has just said, We're out of milk, Dad, the kids are hungry. In the kitchen the baby wails as he is passed around; the sun is now high outside, dropping across the draped window casings. Grant cannot answer, even though he knows she is very frightened and wants to know what is happening and where her mother has gone. After a while, Leila shrugs bravely and says, "I'm takin' us to Muellers'."

He looks through the window and watches as they settle the baby in his stroller, Scott holding his bear, and the four of them head down the gravel road. He watches until the grassland heaves one last time and swallows his children into the black earth.

Grant's open mouth is caked, his lips tight, his teeth glazed like china; he feels as if he's got no defense against the hot air, as if his mouth and nose are just holes in his skull. He moves finally because his bladder is full, has been full for hours, but he's afraid to draw himself up to full height because of what she might have taken away. He reaches through his fly and feels as if she's made his prick skin into feathers; she's hollowed him out from the very point of his penis right up into the hard knot of his gut.

It's noon now, twelve hours since she backed the old Buick out onto the country road. She's a small woman, thin and taut; pregnancies have made her stomach wiry, not loose, but wiry like long scars. She's a fine-looking woman but her teeth aren't good. The big car makes her look foolish, but there's no room for him as she throws it into reverse. She is crying the whole time, but she's also gone. Her breath is always stale from smoking, and when she's in Philip she goes to her friend Martha's room and they drink Canadian Club. She has a good time but she comes back just the same. She's sleeping somewhere now, maybe at a scenic turnoff with the doors locked, or maybe she's driven down into a creek hollow where there are trailers beached like rafts on palm stones. Maybe while she sleeps there will be a flood of yellow waters under a cracked sky.

Grant is back in his chair, but now he's thinking about his dead father, and before long Grant sees him. The whole room smells of him, the cold cattle blood he brought home under his fingernails every day from the yards, ten crescents of decay. He's wearing his overalls, worn to the white warp everywhere but the pencil pocket. His neck is long, and bunches into dark sinews as it slides into his shirt. He walked five hundred miles in the furrows before he was fifteen; they changed teams at either end, but the boy held the reins all day and he walked alone so long that he learned to hear the voices in the ripping sound of parting roots; he walked in the furrows so much as a child that he tripped on smooth floors as a grown man, even years after the farm was lost.

Seems to me, boy, you got some things to attend to.

Grant nods; he'll do anything not to meet that gaze of the father he loved. When he seemed beaten by life and by cancer, his look burned with coal fires, as if he'd been there before and would come back again. Grant would do anything to finish it, to be done with him for good.

How long can you last out here like this? A couple of days? A week?

He gets up at last and looks at his watch for the first time that day: it's almost three. He's hungry, and he goes into the kitchen and tries to find something to eat, not just something, but something good to eat.

There's nothing, just some American chop suey left over from the night before, a few hours before she opened her thighs for him and then stopped him and then was gone. He steps through the back door and out into the dusty yard. He doesn't know who owns this place or any of the land around it; the owner probably doesn't know he owns the place. Grant sends his rent to a lawyer in Pierre. It doesn't matter, the place was Grant's, and could have been always, but Lonnie missed the birds out here on the grassland, that's what she said. She missed the sound of birds, the wave of wind through leaves, she missed the sound of people just passing the time.

He goes inside to the bedroom, gets dressed, and then walks back to his truck. He pulls around halfway into the garage, and then crawls under the camper top to off-load his welder and his tools. He brings one of the mattresses from the kids' room and lays it out in the bed of the truck, and follows with a pile of blankets and pillows. He makes up a box of canned food and juice from the pantry and throws in a handful of knives and forks. He doesn't really know what clothes the kids wear, but he does the best he can into four shopping sacks. He gets his razor. He gets his gun. He takes one last look around the house and then drives off.

Muellers' is about two miles down the road, in a slight hollow that shields them from the worst of the winds but gathers the frost like low fog. It's a big house, two floors and a porch, built by a farmer back when they thought bluestem grass could survive the winter.

Grant drives up and Tillie meets him on the porch. "They're havin' supper," she says.

"I'm leaving Leila with you."

"I cain't take no babies," says Tillie. She's not as old as she thinks, but she's telling the truth.

"That ain't the plan," Grant answers. "Just my oldest." Tillie nods and the flesh bunches around her chin; she's gotten fat out here, that's what happens to good women when the kids are grown—they just keep cooking the same as before.

"I'll explain myself to Hans," he adds.

Grant waits on the porch. He listens to his children finishing their supper and tells himself he's got nothing to be ashamed of.

"Evening, Grant," says Hans, passing him a bottle of his best ale.

Grant takes it, and takes the plate of pork chops that Tillie brings out to him. They sit on the porch; it's good to the west, clear and bright.

"I need a hundred, Hans," says Grant.

Hans goes back into the house and brings back three hundred. It's not kindness, it's just what it takes. Inside, Tillie is running a bath.

"This happens out here," says Hans. "Sometimes the women can't see beyond the day-to-day. I can't tell you why."

Leila comes out to the porch, she's got too much burden on her just now to cry or to be frightened. "Tillie wants to know if you want them in pj's," she says, and Grant nods.

Grant sees Tillie walking over to the truck from the back door and watches as she gathers the four sacks of clothes and carries them back to the house. She's getting a limp and Grant knows it's her hip, just like his mother. He hears the washing machine start up, and sits while Hans smokes his pipe, and then hears the clanking of overall buckles in the dryer. Pete and Scott come out, and they're excited about sleeping on a mattress under the pickup cover. Scott has his teddy bear, and he's telling Teddy all about it, about how maybe they're going to Disneyland, which makes Grant think he may cry yet in front of Hans. Instead, it's Tillie on the lawn who brings a Kleenex to her eyes, and she draws Leila back, right under her bosom, and crosses the loose flesh of her biceps over the girl's soft cheeks. The baby is running hard back and forth over the lawn, and each time he makes a circuit he pats one of the truck wheels. "My turk," he says.

Leila helps them pack the clothes up again, and Hans brings his Coleman stove from the barn. They get the baby into the car seat in front, and the two big boys onto the mattress. Grant hugs Leila, but she's still afraid of love, still too brittle to let herself bend and knows it, even though Grant's been good to her and will always. He starts the truck up and sees Hans listening carefully at the engine, until he's sure he likes what he hears, because everything has to be smooth out here, the rhythm of a day's work that leaves enough for tomorrow, and tomorrow.

"Sometimes," says Tillie, "God just wants to make sure He's got your attention, is all."

Grant nods and backs out. It's a clear night, but there's enough rain in the sky to bring out the musty acid of the grass. It's sharp on his nostrils, but clean; he thinks he can trust it. He turns for Nebraska even though the hunter in him shouts, *Why are you going south? She went west, she's trying to outrun us to the mountains.* Grant looks back through the sliding window into the camper; the older boys are asleep now. It's in their blood to feel comfortable on the road, like Grant's great-grandfather, who left his first, maybe even his second, family and jumped off from St. Louis and went all the way to the Pacific before he turned around back to Nebraska. He arrived in time to gather in the farms the first wave had won and lost, the wives mad, the husbands strangled with worry, the children sick and ancient.

Grant is tired, but the baby is alert in his car seat, his large blue eyes shiny. "See big turk," he says as a triple rig blows past. They've come down the Interstate to Murdo, and are now heading south again toward Rosebud. Grant doesn't want to camp in the reservation, he's hoping to get across the border and stop outside Valentine. He's nodding a little, so he says, "Lots of fun," to the baby. "See Auntie Gay."

"See Mommy."

"Well, that's the thing," he answers, and he realizes he hasn't, in all this time, really thought about *her*, about Lonnie. He can't start now; he can't think of the sharp line of her jaw, or her easy laugh in bed. The baby is asleep now, his lower lip is cupped open like a little spoon. Grant crosses the Nebraska line, and he pulls into the first creek bottom he finds. He finds a level place to park under the steep sides of a sandhill, and carries the sleeping baby around to the back. He pushes Scott and Pete to one side, takes a moment to piss, and crawls in beside them. He can feel their three hot bodies, Grant and his boys curled together. He doesn't know if this will ever happen again, or what will see him through the next few days, or whether his family will ever again be whole.

Everyone wakes crying, even Grant. The baby is soaked, and the air in the camper is strong with the smell of urine and shit. Scott's whimpering for Mommy. Grant sets up the Coleman stove and starts to warm up two cans of corned beef hash, and Pete says, "Where's the ketchup. We always have ketchup."

"There ain't no ketchup," says Grant.

"I don't want to be here," the boy whines, and that starts another round of tears from the other kids. "I want to go home."

They eat, even without ketchup, and that makes everybody feel better. Grant sends Scott and Pete off to the small creek to rinse off the dishes and the frying pan, and when they come back he leads them off a bit behind an outcropping of sandstone and tells them to squat and poop. They think this is funny, and so does the baby, who joins them in the line and pretends to push as the other two drop hot brown fruit onto the dry soil. They're back on the road, all four of them in the cab, a few minutes later, driving down the wide main strip of Valentine. They turn east, through Brown County, then Rock, and Holt. There are so many cars and trucks on the road that the baby kicks his feet with excitement; the boys keep asking him what color they are and he says, Red, and they laugh. There are so many pheasants along the road that Grant thinks for a moment of his shotgun, almost as if this was the hunting trip he'd always planned to take when they got older.

They pick up the Elkhorn River at Stuart and follow it down into O'Neill, where they stop and eat at McDonald's. It's as good as Disneyland for the boys; they each come out holding the plastic sand buckets and toys that came with the Happy Meals; by now they've figured out they're going to Grandma's. Grant wants to tell them what his father said years ago: these places suck the spirit right out of you. Grant was an eager boy then, but he knew his father was telling him this because they'd lost the ranch and now they were moving back to live with his mother's family.

It's Grant's sister Geneva who comes to the door when he rings, and she tries not to look surprised. His ma used to say to him, "It ain't Gennie's fault she was born without the gift of laughter." She's so slow unlatching the screen that Grant thinks maybe she isn't going to, but Scott and Pete have already run around to the tire swing they remembered in back, and it's just Grant holding the baby.

"We didn't hear about this new one," she says. She doesn't ask about Lonnie; just the sight of Grant tending the youngest tells her she isn't with them.

"I'm leaving the kids here for a few days."

Grant knows she's about to say he can't leave no baby with them, but just then his ma comes around the corner pushing her walker. She's shrinking, as if she's just folding together through her disintegrating hips, but she's tough; she's sheltered Geneva all these years. She's got room under those frail arms. Grant leans down to give her a kiss, and she smells like ashes.

"Where's Lonnie?" she asks.

"She's left me. I'm taking the baby to Gay's," he says.

"That ain't going to work," his ma answers. "She's alone now, too."

The baby squirms in his arms, and finally works himself upside down, reaching for the floor.

"Put him down," his ma says. "There's no fire in the stove. No one delivers coal anymore." The baby comes over to the walker and slams his small hand on the tubing, and then starts to climb.

His ma brightens, but this gives Geneva her chance. "We can't keep no baby."

Grant goes out to the truck and brings back two of the remaining three bags of clothes. They still smell fresh from Tillie's dryer, all folded and carefully placed, even though they've been knocked around some. He looks to either side, at the other green lawns and pleasant houses on this quiet, tree-lined street. He doesn't know how his ma did this, how she kept the house after the meat-packing plant was locked one night without word from the owners. Two days earlier the steers had stopped coming in, and when they had split and carved their way through the emptying stock-yards, there was nothing more to kill.

Grant takes a nap in the back room, the vacant sleep of townspeople; his dreams are wild, but they don't mean anything. He wakes drugged but rested, and he eats supper with his ma while Geneva gets things ready for the boys to stay. "Go home, Grant," says his ma. "Go home and wait. You can't take the baby with you. Gay can't and Gennie won't keep him."

He knows she's right. He can't take his baby with him, but he can't wait either, because there is another baby that will need him when he finds Lonnie, a baby that may have to die anyway, but will most certainly not live if he waits for her at home. He says his good-byes to the boys and gives Geneva fifty dollars. His ma works her way out to the truck and watches him put the baby back into the car seat. She's standing there as he drives away, with the baby waving both hands, fingers straight out and spread like two small propellers. "Bye, bye," he sings. "Bye, bye."

They're back out into the farmland in a few minutes, retracing their way toward Valentine. He's still fevered from his nap, and even though he keeps shaking his head and has the windows wide open to the chilly air, his eyes feel puffy and heated. The baby's content to ride high in his car seat, looking around at the land as they begin to roll into the sand hills. Grant doesn't know how he's going to work this: when he finds Lonnie she'll see the baby and that may be the end of it right there, because two hours before she left, the baby had brought her to tears, had finally made her understand that never again in her whole life would something happen easy, that she would forever be fighting just to get through the day. And Grant had tried to comfort her first with love, and then sympathy, and then passion, and it had not worked.

"Piece of milk," the baby sings. Everything from him is melody.

Grant reaches down for one of the bottles he filled at his ma's. "No one wants you," he says to the baby.

"O-kay," he sings back, unblemished.

"No one but me," says Grant finally, and he gives him one of his large round fingers to hold, and the baby drinks his bottle and falls asleep like that. When Grant gasses the truck in Valentine he puts him in back. The little warm head rolls into the soft of Grant's neck; there's a firmness about this body, an energy even when so completely at rest. This time he remembers to put on a dry Pamper, and then checks to make sure the screens on the sliding windows are strong and secure, and locks the tailgate from the outside.

It's two in the morning when he crosses back into South Dakota. The grass doesn't speak to him any-

more, Grant's at peace in the cab with his sleeping
baby behind him. He knows Lonnie can be saved, he
knows this now for the first time, as he and the baby
dart back across the Rosebud Reservation. He sees the
contempt that comes to his sister Geneva's eyes when
she thinks of Lonnie, and he knows why he loves Lonnie, because she's chosen the living, the light. She's
not a whore, she did not become a whore on the plains;
she became a mother. And she was not a whore when
they met, in Pierre, just a nineteen-year-old from east
river who had enough fire and humor not to panic
when she was dropped by her boyfriend hundreds of
miles from home. Grant was twenty: what difference
did it make that they left the Elkhorn bar an hour later
and he wasn't even trying to cover up the erection
stretching his jeans but wearing it out there for every
man to see and to wonder what it would feel like to
slip, once again, into a young body that was bony and
tense and shivering with desire. What difference did
it make that she was pregnant with Leila when they
got married in Philip, in the lobby of the Gem theater
because the usher was the only justice of the peace
who wasn't hunting. After the ceremony, if he wanted
to call it that, they went to Marston's store and were
invited to pick a few things off the shelf, free, and all
Lonnie wanted, or thought she should have wanted,
was a giant-sized box of Pampers.

Grant pulls over finally behind the fairgrounds in
White River and wakes up the next morning to the
baby's big grinning face. "Daddy, Dad-dee," he says,

pounding on Grant's back. They stop at a café for breakfast—he doesn't have the time to cook out anymore—and Grant feels a little funny there with the baby among the farmers and the road crew, as if they thought he was half man, and it hasn't really occurred to him he'll need to bring or ask for some kind of special seat for the baby. But the waitress is older than she looks, she gives the baby a handful of coffee stirrers to play with, and they are back on the road fast and up on the Interstate by ten, heading west.

He hopes to make Sheridan by mid-afternoon, then up into the Bighorn and through the Crow Reservation before he sleeps again. In front of them the grassland buckles and slides, building for the Black Hills. The baby gets restless and starts to cry and then scream, and Grant lets him out of the harness. It's the tourist route, and there are billboards for Wall Drug and the Reptile Gardens, and exit signs for the Badlands and, later, for Mt. Rushmore. He knows she's been this way, he knew it before he started, but now he feels it.

They're in Wyoming, coming first into Beulah and now into Sundance. Grant wonders what the people who started this town were thinking of when they named it Sundance. He knows what it stands for: he's heard the stories about ghost dancing and the sun dance, about men stitched to buffalo skulls with pegs through their breasts. He knows what it stands for, but he doesn't know what it means; no one does, maybe not even the Indians, maybe not even the Indians who danced. It was something for the spirit, not the body;

it was too powerful, and forbidden, nothing like this town that is so quiet a generation could live and die before anyone noticed.

He has to stop a few times at rest areas to let the baby run around, and at Gillette he buys a grab bag full of small toys, and a long tube of Dixie cups that he hands back one by one through the window for two hours until the whole camper is covered with them. "Nother cup!" squeals the baby with delight and surprise, each time. Grant's begun to catch the rhythm of the two-year-old. He wishes he didn't have the baby with him for this last dash to the mountains, but as long as he's got him, he's grateful for the company, for a pal. Grant's got his friends stretched across the plains: they'll never leave the plains. But maybe he's never had a buddy, and maybe he's never guessed that a baby could be a buddy, willing and cheerful to go along, always surprised by events. The land is getting drier, baked hotter over the shining stones and the white rim of alkalai at the waterlines. Lonnie is headed for the mountains, just the way the wagon trains kept the mountains ahead of them, no one worrying about snow in the high passes. Nothing was more foreign to them than the plains. At night, they sang their hymns and hoped the sounds carried beyond the glow of the campfires. They knew they were up against something on the plains. Something that, if they chose to wrestle, they would never be able to let go. He drives past a car wreck and it's a terrible one, two bodies laid out under tarpaulins, casualties on the way to the Bighorn.

This is how it was told to him, like every schoolchild—that Custer would be alive today if he had stayed in South Dakota, but he was teased deeper and deeper into the grass. And it was the same for Lewis and Clark, led by the trapper Charbonneau, but they had a girl with them, an Indian girl, a sign of love and the promise of a gift. She was pregnant just like Lonnie, and it must have been pain, pain beyond the reckoning even of Indian fighters from Virginia, that Captain Lewis and Captain Clark saw the night she gave birth to the child.

In Sheridan, a long hot strip, they stop, and they split a meat-loaf-and-gravy supper at a café and then he gives the baby a bath in the men's room sink of a gas station next door. Grant has never before seen how that skin shines like silk; he traces a line down the flexing back and it feels like powder. Grant uses every muscle and nerve ending in his own body, as if keeping the baby from falling is the one job in his whole life that truly matters. He's toweling him off on the curb outside when he breaks away, naked and round-bellied, to the front, and three high school girls who are gassing a big new Pontiac catch him and bring him back. All three are a little too heavy, and Grant thinks of them as pregnant. They're giggling with the baby and he's giggling back, but when they try to flirt with Grant they read something on his face that chills their laughter, and they hand the baby back to him and leave fast.

That night they sleep in Montana under a few cottonwoods that have found water somewhere deep. He's so tired when they pull in he doesn't notice a small house not much more than a hundred yards away. In the low yellow light of morning an elderly Indian couple appears at his side, just as he and the baby are finishing breakfast. He's made a kind of high chair out of rocks with a scrap of sheet iron as a table. The Indians don't say anything, and Grant guesses this means they're still inside the reservation. Off in the distance a dove is cooing and there is a flapping of laundry in the slight breeze. It's a little chilly and Grant has on a sweatshirt, but the Indians are bundled up as if for winter, the man in an orange nylon parka shiny with dirt and the woman in a heavy blanket jacket over jeans. Grant wonders why they're out at this early hour, but he straightens from his kneeling position in front of the baby when he notices them, and goes over to join the man at the truck while the woman comes over to the baby.

The old man points with a stubby damaged finger toward the baby; the woman is poking at him, taunting him with a piece of bread in a way that is not cruel but not kind either, a test, more like, the first of many. The baby laughs, and the woman swats his head. Grant stiffens; any more of this and he'll spring.

"Yours?" asks the man, and it is as if they're going to fight over the child, not because the Indians want him, but because he's theirs anyway.

Grant looks hard into the old man's face. "That's my boy, my youngest."

"Where's his mama?" the Indian asks. "Where's his grandma?" It's the right question to ask, Grant can't fault it. By now, the baby has finished his breakfast. The woman has freed him from the pile of rocks and they're pitching small pebbles at each other. She's keeping him on the very edge between delight and fear, on the blade of some plan.

Grant doesn't answer; he looks over the Indian's shoulder at the house. There's an old tractor, a Ferguson or a Ford painted hunter green, and it's plain it hasn't run in years. A sprinkler is watering a brown patch of grass.

"We're going after his mama," says Grant, finally. "I can't tell you where she is."

The Indian nods, and then does something that takes Grant by surprise: he picks up Grant's box of Frosted Flakes and eats a couple of large handfuls. Grant doesn't know if he's being robbed somehow, but it doesn't seem necessary for him to say anything. The woman has taken the baby's small hand, and she's leading him down the road to the house. It's flatter here than home, and drier; it's sage country, not grass. On the horizon he can see a straight line of trees, aspens waving a silver flash of leaves, and he knows it's the Bighorn, where the brown trout are big as salmon, where the rainbow males fight each other for the hook. Grant and the Indian follow along, because the woman's in charge now. They go into the small house, two worn steps off the prairie, a shell of gray asbestos shingles, and it's clean, spare, and dark. The baby lets out a squeal of joy when the woman shows him a toy box in one corner filled with trucks and alphabet blocks. They drink coffee.

"How long you planning to look?" asks the man.

"She's headed for the mountains. I'm not far behind."

The woman holds out her arms toward the baby. Grant looks at her for a few seconds before he understands what she is saying: she thinks he's going to leave the baby with them. She thinks it's her duty; she thinks Grant hasn't got the right to refuse.

"We'll be leaving now," he says. He looks over at the baby in the corner and gets ready to cut off the woman's approach.

The man looks at his wife; this isn't his affair, it's up to her.

Grant hears the laundry outside and thinks the pulse of his blood is pounding as loud. He knows he could leave the baby with these people. He's lived his life believing that he could ask anything of Plains people, white or Indian, just the way he knows he'd do about anything if another asked him. He could leave the baby and know he was safe. But he also knows now he can't go on alone. He's too frightened of failing: how does he expect to find Lonnie, a single lungful of air in a sandstorm? How does he think he can do it alone?

Grant pulls out his wallet and gives the woman a ten. He means "Thank you," and he means "No thanks." He's not at all sure that she will take it, but she does, and then she and the man watch as he goes over and picks up the baby, who's having fun with the blocks, and he starts to shriek, beating his arms and legs so fast that for a second Grant almost loses his grip. The baby is reaching out over Grant's shoulder for the toys, he wants those more than anything in the world. The baby screams, "Want Mommy, want Mommy," and Grant knows he's just saying this as a way of getting the toys, but still, it helps, because that's what they're doing. They're going to find Mommy. Grant jogs back down the road toward his truck without looking back for the Indians, and he has to fight hard, harder than he would have imagined, to get the baby buckled into his car seat. He's still screaming; it's been twenty minutes. If Grant tries to keep his children together by himself, it will be Leila, the oldest, who pays the price, but he hasn't asked himself these questions yet. He's only trying to figure out how he'll bring their mother back.

But now they are out on the road, gathering speed. That's all the baby wanted, just some action, something to see or do. Grant feels light, as if they have made an escape, have weathered a close call together.

"You and me, boy, almost got scalped."

There's something about those words that sets the baby off, laughing and laughing. The sound fills the cab, and for a moment they're not in a Ford truck anymore, but Grant doesn't know what it is; he's into his fourth day beyond tired, but he's sharp. He knows he can find her. He feels low and close to the ground, the way a hunter wants to feel when he's caught up at last to the buck in the brush. There's a voice in the deer that tells you where he's going, said his father; it's the way of nature. Close your eyes and listen, that's what his father said, reminded him, on cold fall mornings. But be wary: there are voices outside that are not to be trusted. His father did not say this, but gave witness to it.

Lonnie is running to the northwest; she's a creature of hills and mountains and trees, doing anything not to get caught flatfooted on the plains where the dogs, those endless nameless dogs, can pull her down by the hamstrings. Grant pushes down on the accelerator and the Ford buckles and gulps. He wonders about the old Buick; how long before it dies? He's been looking for it already by the side of the road, in the repair yards of the gas stations, behind the bait-and-tackle shops. He can picture it halfway into the parking lot of a bar just at a place where the men fan out to give her advice, with their eyes all over her ass and crotch, and he knows she feels them looking and it gives her a dot of pleasure and a line of wetness. Maybe she'll decide, Screw it, and they will all head back in, and even the last of the men funneling in the door six, seven behind feels as if he's got something loose on the line. Grant can picture all that because he's never known anything in his life better than Lonnie asking him to turn off the radio and come in and fuck her.

He's looking for her already; when her face comes out to him he won't be surprised. She's stopped running, he knows that because he feels the tiredness in his own body. They come into Billings, past the refineries and tank farms. There is a whole yard full of silver tank trucks, and he says to the baby, "Trucks. See the bi-ig trucks." Grant looks over and sees a wide smile, pure wonderment on that tiny face, and he cannot resist rubbing the backs of his fingers on that round cheek. He thinks if he finds Lonnie, and she comes back with him, looping around through Nebraska to pick up Scott and Pete and then up to Muellers' for Leila and then home, if they all come back to that empty house tired but glad to be off the road, everyone will have won.

They come to a stoplight in the corner of town and now he's got to make up his mind: west or north? He could head west on Route 90 and hit Bozeman and Butte and Deer Lodge and Missoula, one after another. For this reason Lonnie might have taken this route, but the voice inside him says, *No, she went north,* and anyway, if she has a plan, it's to get up to Glacier and look for a waitressing job where they wouldn't suspect or care that she'd run out on a husband and family. That's what she was doing nine years ago when she stopped in Pierre, running out on her parents on the way to Glacier, and the thought never died.

So he heads north out of Billings toward Roundup, and in a few minutes he knows he's done the right thing, because the road's begun to climb, not steep and quick like the push over the Black Hills, but patiently, cutting through the choppy sides of the buttes and the caked bottoms of the valleys. He's crossing the

Musselshell and the Flatwillow, and he sees they're faster and cleaner than the rivers of South Dakota, and he feels their tug back to the east. He is so glad now that the baby is with him that he starts singing "Wheels on the Bus" to him. He doesn't know any of the words, but he's listened to Lonnie sing this song to four different babies and he's got a general idea how it goes. The baby falls asleep. He drives past the town of Grassrange and sees three women tending thrift shop tables in the swirling red dust of the roadside. Each hill rising carries them away from the real earth. Grant feels no mystery in this land, just danger. And when finally, about eleven in the morning, he turns west from Lewistown, he thinks first that it's clouds he's seeing, or a streak of grime cutting across his windshield, but it's neither. He follows the shadows to the left, and to the right, and they're everywhere, mountains beginning to rise out of his life on walls a thousand feet high. They are immense, a shattered warning. He feels the pain the mountains cause, and he knows now that he must find her soon.

He pulls over and slides out of his seat onto the narrow shoulder. The road is high here; before him the foothills swell and mound. There is no traffic, no sound of engines, nothing around except for a gusting wind that pulls at his shirttails and chills the moisture of his sweaty T-shirt. He starts to eat a sandwich he bought in Billings, but he is suddenly too tired to chew. He moves around to sit on the front bumper, out of the wind, and stares west. Maybe Lewis and Clark sat on this spot. They too would have been afraid, because in all this thrusting rock what they had to find was a single drop of water, a single drop that would become two, a puddle, a pool, a stream, a creek, a tributary, and finally a river flowing west. They found it, Grant knows, because they listened to their fear, and the sound that came to them was a waterfall.

She's frightened now, and so is he. He imagines the deer, steamy yellow froth dripping from its sharp lips. He listens for the voice through the whimpering of the grass, through the deep pounding of his heart. She's tired now, he knows that; Lonnie's getting to where she thought she wanted to be, and she's missing her babies, and she knows she lost part of her mind back there on the plains and can't trust what's left. He stands up. He shouts, the words breaking off from the very bottom of his throat, "Where is she?" but this time there is no sound from the grass, just a steady wind. "Where are you?" he yells. The shout is cut off clean; it doesn't even stir the baby. Grant is in the hills now, listening only to the fear that he may have lost Lonnie for good.

Lonnie's purse and wallet are emptied into a small pile in the center of a stained, knobby bedspread. Outside her motel window there is a gas station, and then a lube shop, and then the whole long studded string of 10th Avenue. It's Great Falls, and she cannot believe she has come so far for this, a baked island of neon. The boys she saw last night, bunched into small packs outside the bars, wore the look and hair of the Air Force. Some of them spoke to her as she walked into what was left of the old cow town, past nameless markers and corners that were nothing but numbers. She could get work here; tonight she can be inside some bar wearing a white cowboy hat and fringed hot pants, and if that's all she does, it will last for two or three months, until one late afternoon the satin waistband no longer closes at the snaps. Already she feels the force inside her: sooner, more powerful, more demanding than any of the others, so strong that it pushes the others aside, her real babies whose soft skin and voices she misses so badly that her arms ache.

She could get work here, and she'd ask the other waitresses who to talk to about fixing everything; maybe it wouldn't cost anything, maybe the state would pay for it. She could do this, it's what she planned. All the way from home, eyes on the mirror for the growing red dot of Grant's truck, she pictured the nurse, bored maybe and unforgiving, working through a list of questions as if it were a driver's-license renewal or one of those customer-service people doing interviews in the I.G.A. And then there would be a white room, and a white sleep, and it would be done. It wouldn't be so bad, really. In a few days it would all be over, and then, then she might think about going back.

She counts sixty-four dollars, and change. She has a full tank of gas, and even though the Buick has started to skip a little and lose power, she knows enough to guess it is just the altitude, the thin air. Her clothes are clean; earlier that morning she met a woman at the motel's coin-op, a tourist from Oklahoma washing out a few kids' T-shirts, and she offered to let Lonnie throw in her things because the machine wasn't hardly full. She was the kind of person Lonnie had often wished could be her neighbor, in a house that didn't exist and would never, she knew, have a reason to be built.

Grant may still be back home; if he is, she hopes he's thought of Tillie Mueller to help him, but it's all just wishing. He's hunting her because he thinks it's his duty, and she's not afraid of what would happen if he finds her, she's just afraid of being hunted, the seeker already tugging on her from the other side of the plains.

She leaves her motel and begins to walk. She tries not to see what she's seeing, to see any landmarks through her own eyes, because Grant will see them too; she tries not to say the name of this city, because Grant will hear it. When she married him she didn't ask for this, except maybe by wanting something different as a teenager, something with mystery. He has powers; people laugh at her when she tells them that, but it's true, it's always been true. Grant is so thin and blond that people think he's nothing but a kid, until they look him in the eye.

She has lunch, a salad at Burger King. It's her first meal of the day, and the memory of the morning sickness she endured with Leila, and then less with Scott, churns at her stomach. If she wants to find work tonight she'll have to start in a couple of hours, by four at the latest. She doesn't doubt that he knows where she was headed; when she left him she turned without even thinking, and didn't realize she'd gone west until she began to see the signs for Rapid City. She told him she was headed west the night they met in the Elkhorn Bar; her boyfriend got scared and turned back after a last beer together, and then, at that second, the good-bye wave she gave to the old boyfriend turned into a hello to Grant as the two boys passed in the bar door-way. But even if he knows she is in Montana, where will he start? Even if he knows she is in the city whose name she doesn't want to say out loud, can he find her? Even if he knows what block she is on, a block made of avenues and streets that are just numbers, no names at all, what is the chance he'll spot her?

She looks up from the counter in a sudden fright and quickly scans the restaurant. She has to stop think-ing these thoughts, they're energy flowing out of her, a beacon for him. She's giving herself away. She runs outside and cuts off 10th Avenue back toward the old city. She walks until she comes to the Missouri, and she reads a sign that says GIBSON PARK. She brings her hands to her face, because now those words are out on the line and maybe he knows them, maybe he's heard of this place. The grass is green here, and there are children in the play yard and a few old men pitch-ing horseshoes. She doesn't think of the trees or the statue she's standing in front of, or the white, freshly painted bench she has to sit on for a minute or two, because her legs are fluttering. Why wouldn't he let her be? Why couldn't he give her some time, such a small amount of time?

She's walking again, and now she's got a new plan: she'll blank her mind; she's thinking about home, she's going through the drawers of the steel cabinet unit and she's picturing the knives, the forks; she's counting the spoons, including the baby spoon with the chipped plastic handle that has a line of ducks on it, except the yellow paint they used for the beaks washed off. She's trying to count the floorboards in the kitchen, but it isn't working; she's still on that baby spoon. She has held that spoon for four babies, scooped in the first mouthfuls of pears and custard, given those four babies their first tastes of life on that spoon. Even now she can feel through the handle the cleaning tug of the baby's lips when he or she is hungry, and the resistance of the tongue that moves her hand aside when he's not. She's given her children everything on that spoon, and now she wants to hold it and look at those beakless ducks.

When she gets back to the bars, the neon is bright, not because it is dark or will be in three more hours, but because the watch has changed at the Minuteman base and the boys will soon be here. She's standing there, just one of the girls, and a big red pickup goes by and takes a wide U-turn back, and she looks away and says to herself, Please, let it be some ranch hand looking for a whore, but it's not, and she does not ask

herself any more questions about how he did it. He
has dropped down on her through a hole in the day,
a parting of clouds straight up to the sun. He parks
alongside her and comes forward halfway and stands
crazy, so spent that she thinks he will fall, and they
look at each other until it seems that he has started
talking without making a sound.

"Lonnie," he says, "I won't hurt you." There's
gravel in his voice, he's hoarse and it makes her think
he's been crying.

She looks into the truck and sees the baby, who starts
pumping his arms up and down in a little dance, even
though he's still strapped in. "Mommy," he shouts.
She can't help smiling, the baby makes her smile and
laugh for the first time in five days. She can feel the
tug to him, powerful, intoxicating. He's every bit as
demanding as before, as merciless, as selfish as he
reaches, but there's a sweetness now; the difference is
she wants to give it to him, to all the kids, to Grant.
Her body starts flowing toward the baby, her breasts
heavy.

"Oh God, Grant, you brought the baby." As she says
this she pictures the two of them riding in the truck
together, side by side, and remembers how so long ago
she loved to think of him and the kids together.

"I didn't have no choice," he says, but she sees
through it, she knows he couldn't have found her
alone.

"Where are the others?" It is suddenly agony to be
apart from them.

"Carry!" yells the baby from the truck. "Carry," he yells again, reaching out, and she can feel herself open for him, a torrent now, a cloudburst.

"They're safe. Do we still have another coming?"

"I can't have another. I can't do it. You can't make me."

"I want you back. I need you back."

"You can have me back, Grant. I want to come home. I miss my babies." She's trying not to cry. She's Lonnie, she's only twenty-nine, she has come to this place and cannot escape. "But this child will kill me."

And Grant has known for five days that he can come this far and no farther. He'll choose the living, he'll choose Lonnie. And Lonnie has known for five days that whether she likes it or not, Grant and her babies are everything for her, that she wants nothing else. She is crying now as she passes Grant on her way to the truck. She picks up the baby and he feels like satin, and the three of them stand for a moment on this spot in this city beside the Missouri River. Lonnie thinks of the river on the map, flowing north out of Great Falls almost to Canada before it begins to drop southeast, straight back home through South Dakota. They could almost ride home on a raft.

A Gracious Rain

ONE EARLY SUMMER EVENING, Stanley Harris, a family man with a wife named Beth, sat on his porch and looked out idly as two clergymen went about their separate and competing duties among their parishioners on Raymond Street. To Stanley's eyes it was a pleasant scene. The red sun brought colors out of the brown lawns and weathered clapboards, and the low shafts of light played and wound through the repetition of porches, stoops, and gables. In the evening, the rich smells of frying pork and fresh dinner rolls replaced the dust of midday and the chaff from the grain elevator. Stanley listened to the sharp yips of the children playing, and the low mumble of their parents sharing their days, and he reflected that, considering the choices, he could have met a worse fate than to live and die on a back street in Cookestown, Maryland.

This evening's pastoral duties, performed by Father William Francis, pastor of Immaculate Conception, and Dr. Emmett Daggett, of the Second Baptist, could not be called momentous. Father Francis helped Gladys Foster into the car for a visit to her sister Ethel in the hospital, and then walked quickly to the Smarts' to discuss, Stanley was sure, altar flowers. Dr. Daggett ran gamely to field a wild pitch, clutching his glasses, cross, and pocketful of change, but otherwise seemed to have little on his schedule. It was enough for him to stand there, gold teeth shining in his black face like the cross on his dark suit, reminding his flock of the Word. Stanley and his family were Episcopalians, "Anglicans," his mother used to say, tracing an alleged lineage back to families fleeing from Oliver Cromwell. But he had no quarrel with Father Francis or Dr. Daggett, even if he found the Catholic a little stiff for his taste. He rather liked the feeling that Raymond Street attracted this kind of attention, like the occasional pass down the street by Officer Stapleton that made him feel noticed and well served.

When Stanley was in the Army, in Germany during the Johnson buildup, he'd often been struck with much the same feeling. Most of the Army seemed dedicated to feeding him, maintaining his very nice teeth, entertaining him with movies and occasional USO shows; that the cooks and dentists and musicians avoided their share of all-night field exercises didn't strike him as unfair given the gifts of a hot meal and a painless mouth to eat it with. Even in the field the Army was thoughtful enough to supply cigarettes in the K rations; though Stanley didn't smoke, he had traded the Marlboros for canned peaches.

Stanley worked as a machinist at the Jones Machine Tool plant in Easton, and often came home with feathery spirals of stainless steel caught in his hair. He knew enough to appreciate this job, in a plant that had landed as if from nowhere in a played-out cornfield. Why would a company that big put a plant in Easton? How would they know Easton existed? He was proud to walk into his shop every morning under a banner that read *The Jap invasion stops here.*

In fact, when the rector of their church, the Reverend James Broadhurst, said that, even as Christ had, we would all die feeling forsaken, Stanley could not help but take silent and prayerful issue. Stanley admired Mr. Broadhurst's words, but the priest always wore a rather whipped-dog look on his frail brow, and seemed eager to hear of his flock's deepest doubts. Maybe it was because the still-young preacher had no wife and lived alone in an old huntsman's cottage at the tip of Spears Neck. The sound of all those geese in the winter would drive anyone crazy. So when Mr. Broadhurst preached about the universal fear that God would forget us, Stanley listened gravely but saved his real fear for himself: that God would remember him all too well, that He already had blessed him. But why? Why would He bother?

"What you thinking about so hard there," asked Beth, who'd come out for a cigarette and breather. She liked to lean against the porch rail with her back to the last cusp of sun, the fires of daylight turning brilliant on the distant waters of the Bay. Stanley had always thought the homes of Raymond Street, built by a mill gang in the thirties, looked like houseboats, one by one, long and narrow, with overhanging roofs to keep the sun off vacationers. In the dim light, Stanley could see Beth, thicker now after her pregnancies but still fit, her straight brown hair in the same bob she'd worn since high school, and he saw her leaning over the rail of a houseboat, like girls in the travel ads of the *Register*. Susan, Timmie, and Molly were in the bath. Behind Beth, Delia Bagwell was calling the kids to bed, and behind Bagwells' was McCready, and Twyford, and Pusey. Stanley and Dickie Bagwell had little to say to each other, but Delia and Beth were best friends, close as high-schoolers and so often seen shopping together that newcomers in town mistook them for sisters.

"Nothing," he said. "I was just setting, darlin."

Whenever Stanley tried to explain his deepest thoughts, even to himself, he ended up close to blasphemy, which made him nervous. Yet whenever a feeling of meaninglessness nagged at him, the more he felt chosen to bear witness that life had a reason and a reward, that life was a blessing. At the plant, during coffee, he sometimes tried to interrupt the bitching of his friends with a few words of moderation, and Bobby and Frank were sharp and quick enough to call him "Preacher" because of it. It was not that Stanley didn't complain now and again about the way Beth kept house or the new shop rules. But though he tried, he never could see why the things that didn't work in his life should be so much more important than the things that did. He couldn't seem to lose his temper about any of it, a lack of passion that earned him a reputation as something of a marshmallow when it came to sticking up for his rights. Because he was well liked, he had once been nominated from the floor for union shop steward, a suggestion that was hooted down by his best friends with a lot of fun all around. For a few days after that he worried that maybe it was true, maybe he was a pushover. But in the end, Stanley decided that there was a part of him that sometimes, like tonight, filled his soul with questions so deep that he felt graced to think of them at all. It was a gift, something that he didn't understand very well, and maybe no one would, and maybe it was something that was simply beyond his brain power to grasp or express.

"Night, Dad." Eight-year-old Timmie had come out, clean and sleepy, the way Stanley loved his children best. The last red glow was fading from the horizon. Stanley gathered him in, rubbed his cheek on the boy's soft, aromatic head, and patted his skinny bottom through the spaceman pajamas.

"Say your prayers."

"I hate Susan," said Timmie. Stanley had heard snatches of a fight a few minutes earlier, and he had to admit that Susan, thirteen just last week, was quickly becoming impossible.

"Okay. God will get up and down with Susan," he said, and gave him a final shove back in the door.

It was dark now on Raymond Street; the special restfulness of dusk had ended as the mumble and murmur of games and conversations hushed into individual voices. A baby cried at the west end, probably little Emlen Paggin; and from the other end of the street he heard the sharp bark of a man's "Shit on you," and a door slamming. All over Cookestown, people were drawing away from the dark and dew and into the false light of the houses. Stanley could picture, up and down the street, the husbands and wives grinding toward rapid and silent climax, toward the emptiness of the first hours before dawn. Stanley feared emptiness, the eternal dark, just like everybody. Inside, Beth was beginning the dishes, and he would soon slip in beside her to dry. She would need stories about his day, and though this duty fatigued him more than anything he could imagine, he would do his best. Raymond Street was on its own now: no clergy, no police, just Stanley turning for a final look from the door with the dying wonder of the gift that was his, and was not.

The following morning Stanley woke up feeling not bad, but different. He dressed and ate with a sense of change coming, most likely the beginning of a cold or possibly another bout with his slipped disc. He told himself that this was part of being over forty, the sense that the body was telegraphing its minor disturbances and pains. But no sooner had he punched in at the plant and settled at his lathe than his heart ruptured along an unsuspected family fault line, and he died without catching his breath.

Two hours later, in the white light of mid-morning, when the asphalt and rooftops of Raymond Street were soft, and the dogs under the porches wore fixed grins and boiling eyes, Beth Harris glanced up from folding her laundry as if someone had called her, and looked out the front window. She saw Mr. Broadhurst and Officer Stapleton climbing out of the cruiser. She fell down where she was, in front of the screen door, and the men had to run around back to let themselves in through the kitchen. They rushed over to her, but as they knelt down she jumped up swinging, and nearly connected with Mr. Broadhurst's jaw, and he backed off until he fell into a brown Morris chair.

"So it's yours now," screamed Beth. "It's God's?"

And it took Mr. Broadhurst a few moments to realize she was talking about the chair, but by this time Delia Bagwell had come running with an undiapered baby under one arm, and little Molly began shrieking from her crib. Beth ran to the bedroom while Delia, still holding her own baby on her hip, called Beth's mother, who lived in Chestertown and had no car. At the door appeared a couple of the Paggin girls, one of whom was wearing a purple T-shirt with *Spittle* written on it, and they reached into the room to snatch Molly out of Beth's arms and take her down to the other end of the street. And as all this carried forth Frank Stapleton looked at the clergyman in amazement and said, "Neither of us never said a word."

By two in the afternoon, the Benefits Office had arranged for Stanley to be brought to Lee and Evans Funeral Home, and Beth and her mother went to see him. Beth's cousin Harold, the surliest gas-station attendant in the county, drove her mother over from Chestertown in his Dodge Charger, and despite the occasion laid a patch of rubber on Raymond Street as he left. Her mother was wearing a light blue pantsuit and had brought her white leather purse, but Beth hadn't changed from her jeans and sweatshirt. She borrowed Delia's car, and they passed through town with a procession of clanks, down Raymond Street to Chester, to the courthouse square with its fragrant lines of box bushes, and down past the low whitewashed brick office buildings of Lawyers' Row. She didn't know if Stanley had a will; she didn't know who would know, or if it would ever matter. They stopped at the corner by the school, and Beth began to cry. Timmie and Susan were there, for the annual two-week summer camp organized by the Cookestown United Church Council. "They don't know yet, Mama," she said. "They're in there playing, thinking everything's fine, and their daddy's dead."

Her mother couldn't say anything right, so she told Beth the light was green.

"Shouldn't we stop for flowers or something?" asked Beth suddenly as they drove to a space in front of the

Victorian home of Lee and Evans. "I don't know what to do."

The pink stucco building was hooded with striped awnings on every window. Beth remembered the sign that used to hang on the movie theater marquee: COME ON IN. IT'S COOOOL INSIDE. That was their first date: she wore a yellow muumuu, a tube-like fashion her mother had copied from a picture of Jackie Kennedy, and they saw *Blue Hawaii*, with Elvis.

"Now don't worry about what you do or don't do," said her mother. "Phil Evans said to leave everything to him."

Beth had been schoolmates with Sally Pingree Evans. "It's like she won this time for good."

"Shush. To think of childhood quarrels at a time like this."

"I always had Stan," she said, and she reached into her purse and took out a Kleenex, a comb, and a piece of gum.

Phil Evans met them at the door. To Beth, he had always seemed a little light, a "fairy," but today she found his manner surprisingly soothing. The voice, the eyes, the familiarity—they reminded her that people die all the time, even die young like Stan, and there was no use being ashamed of it. He led them through the offices and past the floral arrangements just delivered for the evening wakes, and into a simple, windowless room where a body lay under a sheet. Phil paused to see whether both women were composed, and pulled back the cover.

And there was Stanley. She reached out immediately, and her hand, by accident, fell right on the long scar from the corner of his left eye. She gasped and pulled her hand back, but whether what shocked her was touching his scar or the unfamiliar feeling of cold flesh, she could not be sure. Some days she'd have to force herself not to look at this blemish when she talked to him; it now seemed so necessary, an identifying mark, as the police said. She didn't know whether she was going to cry or not. Right then, for a second—a flicker as long as the heart attack that killed him—she had to search in her heart to find the love she felt for him, to find the sharp part of it. He had such a good jaw, with those fine teeth that she could see through his slightly parted mouth. Beth used to look at him during sermons, down at the other end of the family pew, and his jaw made him seem so intelligent, as if Mr. Broadhurst were speaking only for him. Beth had never learned how to concentrate on the sermons; by the time one child had reached the age where he or she could be depended upon to sit quietly, another came along. He'd missed a place, that very morning, shaving, and there was a small square of whisker under his chin. Maybe it was only mistakes that outlived people, she thought. He seemed so dead; Beth couldn't help using the word to describe the way his body and limbs looked. Beth could see that the funeral home had already put some powder on his face; it still bore the trace of pain, but the mouth and eyebrows had started to relax as he went down, and the last suffocated breath left him looking strangely content. It was a martyr's face, she thought. It was, she suddenly realized, a message to her from Stan, and at that, tears did begin to come.

"It was very quick," said Phil. "He could not have been in pain."

"I still don't understand," she sobbed. "It was a weak heart or something?"

"You'll have to ask Dr. Peters, Elizabeth." Phil still held the sheet high above Stanley and his arms began to quiver and drop. He did feel professionally competent to add, "His rest is now complete."

"You can put your arms down now," she said, composed again. "It's Stanley."

"Of course," said Phil.

"No," said Beth, looking one last time at that satisfied brow, "I mean, this is how Stanley would have wanted to look."

She left her mother to make arrangements, and retraced her steps back to the front door. Outside she paused to take three or four deep breaths, and to look both ways to make sure no one was coming toward her. Except for the funeral home, no one she knew well would have reason to be in this neighborhood; the cooks and cleaning ladies were all from Corsica Hollow. She began walking toward town, crackling the brittle sheets of plane tree bark that peeled all summer. There weren't any trees on Raymond Street—just a few scrubby privet hedges overgrown with honeysuckle. She'd never lived on a street with trees and now she never would. Not that getting or being rich was anything she and Stanley had thought much about. At the beginning, her mother had argued against Stanley. I don't see much ambition in the boy, said her mother, and she was right if all there was to ambition was wanting something you didn't have. That was fine for Stanley now, but Beth began to worry how long Timmie's sneakers would last and whether his coat from last year would still fit. She couldn't remember if she'd bought underpants for Susan at the K mart yesterday, and if she had, whether Susan would demand some different kind—colored bikinis, maybe—now that she had so many opinions. Molly would be in Susan's hand-me-downs for years, that was okay, but there was no way they could afford Pampers anymore and no way they'd ever see a washing machine in their house, so she just better plan now to be spending a lot more time in the BestClean.

By now she was standing on the hot concrete of the school entrance, a set of stairs rising like bunkers out of the worn brown grass. The building faced the courthouse and was often mistaken for the county jail. Beth was tired now, her legs felt spongy and her breath kept dropping out of the bottom of her lungs. She sat on the steps and lit a cigarette, and listened to the muffled voices of the children playing inside, and the sound farther off of the tomato trucks, loaded to the axles, downshifting into Fox's canning, and then, way in the distance, the faint whine of Route 50, almost bumper to bumper on hot days all the way from the Bay Bridge

A Gracious Rain

to Ocean City. She didn't feel like herself, sitting here only seven or so hours after Stanley had died; she felt she was watching all this from above, as in the movies, as if she had died too and some stand-in was breaking the news to the kids.

At last there was activity from inside the door, a final shout in the hall before the birds flew, and at just the same moment Beth's mother pulled up to the curb in the Bagwells' Dodge. So when Susan came out first, acting so sophisticated with her friends Meg and Tiffany, what she saw was her mother climbing to her feet from the steps, and her grandmother, dressed in a suit with her white purse, getting out of the Bagwells' car, and Susan's bright smooth look was replaced with a scowl, because even as she understood something very bad had happened, she realized also that her afternoon plans were now ruined. But when Timmie ran out a few moments later, his maroon hat pulled over his scarlet hair, his eyes darted from his mother to his grandmother to Susan, and he kept looking for a second for the other person who should have been there given the totally unexpected presence of his mother and grandmother, and he dropped his tin lunch box, and cried out, "Where's Daddy!" And by this time Susan's friends had taken several steps beyond her, and she gave one last look at them as if she had somehow been expelled from the group, and then ran to lead Timmie, whimpering now like a puppy, into their mother's arms.

They drove back to Raymond Street with Beth in

the back seat holding the children, but at the top of the street Beth waved her mother on and they headed out onto the flat of Route 50 and turned south. They all cried a good bit, even Beth's mother as she drove along slowly, mostly in the breakdown lane. Beth watched the trucks thundering by, and looked out at the road crews and farmers deep in their fields, and saw all these workingmen, with wives at home, all still alive. Soon they reached the Bay Bridge, a heaving backbone hunched over the silent water, and Beth tapped her mother on the shoulder. They turned and were nearing their exit when Beth tapped again, and her mother understood and drove into Frostee's Ice Cream. They took a booth, and for a moment all four of them sat in front of their sundaes topped with sharp spirals of whipped cream and they cried once again, as if saying grace.

"Are they sure?" said Timmie finally.

"Yes, hon. Grandma and I saw him."

Timmie picked up his spoon and started on his ice cream, and then asked, "Is he in heaven?"

Beth hesitated, and asked herself what Mr. Broadhurst would say.

"Of course he is," said her mother, glowering at Beth's delay. "He's watching over us right now."

"Oh, Grandma," said Susan.

"Shush," said her grandmother.

They all picked at their sundaes. But it had been the right move, to come into this air-conditioned world surrounded by orange and purple plastic. Everyone there, except for Beth and her mother, was so young, the counter girls not much older than Susan, their round adolescent bottoms straining in the purple short-shorts of the Frostee's uniform.

"Are you going to stay tonight?" Susan asked her grandmother.

Beth glared: Susan was asking whether she would have to sleep on the couch. "We don't know what's going to happen just yet. Eat your sundae."

They all made a last attempt to finish, and then left. From the averted looks Susan got from the high school girls, Beth knew the word had traveled through town. This time when they reached the head of Raymond Street, the light now the burnished yellow of a closing day, there was nothing left but to drive down the center, between the porches. Normally the children would be out by now, darting through the evening like fireflies. But the baseball games of the boys and the curbside Pony and Pound Puppy parties of the girls were off for the night. Instead, there were cars bunched at the middle of the street in front of their house, several strollers—Beth read each of them like name tags—on the lawn, and Nancy Paggin was disappearing in their front door carrying a casserole dish and a bag of groceries topped by a flowering of celery leaves.

A parking space had been left for them at the front, and as the four of them headed up the oyster-shell walk to the house, Beth had the sensation that she was carrying something, like a new television in a big cardboard box, that she wished she could keep private from the neighbors. She took little notice of all the familiar faces. Considering the number of people in their small house, there was surprisingly little noise, but the hot air was fluid and heavy with sweat. They were spread all over the house, into the hall and back to her bedroom, the cousins, the Puseys, McCreadys, and Twyfords.

The family walked in, and one by one they were peeled off, until Beth ended up alone in the kitchen with Delia. Both women burst into tears as they started to hug, and as Beth sobbed she felt the comfort of Delia's breasts and the warmth of Delia's cheek on hers, a softness without whiskers or the smell of work, and she wondered if ever again a man would hold her, or if she wanted it to happen, ever again. At length they parted, and made the apologetic faces two friends make when their cheeks are stained with tears, and Delia turned to stir the chicken stew that had been simmering on the stove all day.

Beth took a moment to herself on the back steps, and then worked forward into the front room. From the doorway she saw Mr. Broadhurst standing quite uncomfortably beside the floor lamp. None of Stanley and her friends on Raymond Street was an Episcopalian, and the day for the parish visit would come later, yet she couldn't help but observe that the one person who should have known what to do looked like the one person someone should send home.

"It's real nice of you to come," she said to him.

He was holding a Dixie cup and had worked his little finger up through the bottom. He blushed slightly as he pulled his hands free, and made a show of crumpling the cup, as if to prove to Beth that he had drunk some wine just to be sociable.

He said, "My place is at your side, Elizabeth," and he reached out for her hand awkwardly, without stepping closer to her, his own hand now unencumbered.

Beth thanked him, for what she wasn't entirely sure, and began to greet the people who had come into her house. The men were still in their work clothes, but most of the wives, unlike Beth, had changed into skirts, put on makeup, and done their hair. The white and black faces mingled comfortably, which was something that might not really happen except for times like this, but could happen anytime, and was comforting to Beth because Stanley would have been pleased. All these people in her house, even the children and babies, all of them would die one day, that was the point; all of them, like Stanley, would go. That's the message, anyway, that Beth took from them. Before she knew it, she had begun to think of each new face she greeted, each new body that embraced her, almost as a corpse. And when she realized this she thought she might faint, and asked Hugh Twyford to take her out for some air.

The day had now cooled into early evening. Susan was already out there sitting with the Paggin girls, and the three of them were playing with Molly. Beth picked up the baby and stood for a long time holding her firm little body, the warmth of her tufted head. "Where's Timmie, sweetheart?" she asked Susan.

Susan didn't know, so Beth sent her off to find him, and a minute or two later she came back to say he was in the bedroom with Mr. Broadhurst.

"What are they doing?" Beth asked.

"They're playing Clue, I think. Something." Susan looked embarrassed. "Timmie was telling Mr. Broadhurst that Daddy's in heaven."

"What did Mr. Broadhurst say?"

"Mom," Susan whined.

"I just want to know whether Timmie needs me."

"Well, I don't know. He's fine." Beth reached out and patted Susan on the head; there just wasn't enough room in there for her father's death, not today anyway.

They fed all the children first, the mothers, some holding babies, standing behind the chairs of the little ones, reaching forward to catch a plastic cup of milk before it flooded the table, and then sent the children out into the sweet dusk of summer with ice cream bars. The adults sat on chairs brought from other houses, in front of dishes and silverware brought from other kitchens. They quieted for Mr. Broadhurst's prayer, which contained a line that we will know God "not by reason but by fire," and as the conversation resumed, Beth heard old Mr. McCready announce that this thought was "too deep by a fathom for me." Then one by one, and family by family, they gathered their things, bid goodbye and courage to Beth, and left. A light rain had begun to fall, and they dashed to the ends of Raymond Street with their chairs and utensils held over their heads. Delia took her place in the kitchen, where she would remain for the next few days, and Beth and her mother put everyone to bed. Susan would sleep with Beth, on Stanley's side, and Beth knew if they woke in the middle of the night they could talk, perhaps even go out to the porch together in their nightgowns and watch the sun rise. She could not have borne Timmie lying there, already such a little male, with his father's sharp features, but she went to his room and lay beside him while he cried, and curled up onto him as he fell asleep.

When all this was done Beth came back out into the quiet house, and was surprised and annoyed to see Mr. Broadhurst's brooding presence leaning against the rail out on the porch. She wasn't sure why he assumed the right to be the last to leave. But Stanley would have wanted this conversation, so she opened the screen door as silently as possible and leaned against the rail on the other side, with Stanley's empty chair between them.

"That was real nice of you to play with Timmie," she said.

"He will do fine. He's very sure his father has been gathered into the fellowship of saints."

"I know," said Beth.

"Stanley was a man of great faith. He had . . . faith . . ." Mr. Broadhurst's thought trailed off.

It was a black night. "Can I get you some coffee?" asked Beth.

"Oh no, Elizabeth. I must be going, of course."

But he didn't go, and Beth was by now fatigued and perplexed. Searching around in her mind for something suitable, she said, "Stanley always loved the line where Jesus says—of course I can't really say it—but he says, 'If it wasn't true I wouldn't say so.' "

"Oh yes. John 14:1–6. 'In my Father's house . . .' "

"He liked it because it seemed so matter-of-fact."

"Yes," said Mr. Broadhurst, but the whole conversation seemed to have depressed him even further. Beth said nothing more, and they both stared out into the darkness of Raymond Street until finally, not a moment before she felt she would simply have to say good night and leave him there, he announced that he must go. He straightened, and then had to maneuver slightly around Stanley's empty chair so that he could draw close to her and once more take her hand, and he held on to it as he said, "We would all like to know the truth, wouldn't we, Elizabeth?"

"The truth?" asked Beth. He still had her hand.

"When it's a man as young as Stanley . . ."

Beth did not understand what he was saying, but she did understand that he wasn't really speaking to her. "I'm sorry," she said finally.

He waved off her sympathy with a joyless smile. "Please remember what I said inside. I am always here for you, and," he added, "the children." Finally he let go and walked quickly through the rain out to his car, and when he turned the key, the radio came alive at the volume he had set on the way over, and it blasted forth a line or two of an advertisement for discount clothing, before he could hastily turn it down.

And Stanley looked on all this with a sense of distance that, under the circumstances, hardly surprised him. He felt extremely bad for Beth, it having fallen to her to deal with Mr. Broadhurst very much as one spouse occasionally must spend a terrible evening with the drunken best friend of the other. If Stanley had thought it mattered, he would have warned her earlier about Mr. Broadhurst's darker side, for his sermons were full of it, full of disciples losing heart, full of the loneliness of Gethsemane. He would do better tomorrow, buttressed by the presence of the vestry and the parish children; he'd be too busy to brood.

On this matter of the hand-holding, however, Stanley was as surprised as Beth. He never would have guessed that Mr. Broadhurst harbored feelings for her, even though, from the inner peace of his current viewpoint, Stanley found Beth almost impossibly lovely in every way. It would be a mistake from the start, not that Beth would make it. But poor old Mr. Broadhurst would: even now, as he drove out Route 16 to his empty cottage on Spears Neck, awash with embarrassment, tormented by something the living called guilt but which Stanley recognized now was the very fire of mortality. He could only follow his headlights, straight ahead into the darkness beyond their reach. From above, Stanley could see the route, out all the way to the cottage, all the way beyond into the Corsica River and out onto the Bay. Mr. Broadhurst would keep driving till he drowned at this rate: she was too much for him, Stanley figured.

Stanley had certainly believed, all his life—he was just getting used to the real meaning of the phrase—that she was too much for *him*. He'd asked her on their first date because Delia Bagwell ordered him to, and they went to the Palace and saw Elvis in *King Creole*, but Stanley had been so nervous he couldn't remember a single frame of the show. He had come home from the Army expecting bad news—he wasn't much of a letter writer—and there she was waiting for him, as he had always believed she would be, against odds that Stanley more than anyone judged overwhelming. Because in that abyss, when all he could picture was her saying "I do" to a hundred more suitable men, a more unlikely and perhaps impossible image grew even more radiant. Hope had kept him going, but it was the doubt that gave him joy.

Stanley, it was true, wished Beth hadn't taken a swing at Mr. Broadhurst, and he found it disappointing that, if only for a moment, she had thought back to her long-running competition with Sally Pingree. On the other hand, he did have to admit to himself that he felt a deep irony when his body ended up on Phil Evans's slab. The man had been patronizing him for years, and actively avoided him on the streets of Cookestown. Who was he to tell Beth that "his rest was now complete"? He was wrong in every way, as if rest was ever anything Stanley had sought anyway.

And who was he to tell Beth that a fatal heart attack is painless? He wouldn't want Beth to know it, of course, but the feeling of a mortal organ virtually splitting in two made childbirth and kidney stones look like a day at the beach. A millisecond of that was enough for eternity.

He wasn't really surprised to see her staring blankly at his body when Phil Evans pulled back the sheet. He might have hoped for a more tender moment, but he had from time to time in the past wondered whether he would cry freely and unselfconsciously if Beth died. Perhaps it had something to do with vanity, a condition, he recognized now, that found expression in the flesh but was not entirely restricted to it. If he had still had his body it would have stiffened when Beth's hand landed on his scar, a jagged blemish that went from the corner of his eye into his hairline. It had bothered him almost from the day Lee McCready did it with a brick when they were eight, an accident that nearly cost Stanley his vision on one side. Sometimes, meeting new people, he had to force himself not to consciously present his good side, keeping the other in a kind of shame. He wondered now, in fact, even after he had left his body behind, whether he would still be known as the "guy with the scar," or maybe, more accurately, as "the guy who used to have the scar."

But it was such a small matter, such an odd little detail, that it did nothing more than give resonance to the thing. In the meantime, he had so much more to think about. Beth. The kids. Yes, those wonderful, sweet children. He was delighted to hear Timmie lecture Mr. Broadhurst that he was in heaven; Stanley was also glad that Timmie would lose his certainty as he aged, because there would be no savor in his life without questions. As Stanley had, Timmie would sit on his porch in the evenings, and wonder. And Susan. Oh, where had the glorious idea for adolescence come from, that magnificent rush, the body searing itself in fullness onto the flesh? If he could, he would have kissed her when she asked Beth's mother whether she was staying for the night; he would carry the image of her frown at the schoolyard forever, even as she grew into womanhood and finally into the decrepitude of age. And could humankind ever condemn itself, could a man find fault with his species once having known a single two-year-old? Molly in some sense that Stanley knew he'd have to figure out, was the Resurrection.

Yes, everything was going fairly much as he might have imagined, except for one large detail: the communion of saints, as he had tried to picture it when reciting the Apostle's Creed, was not exactly complete. In fact, when Mr. Broadhurst had talked about "the eternal fear that God would forget us," he was more correct than he knew. Because everyone around Stanley seemed, just as before, to be waiting, and searching. The babel of complaints and jealousies had survived death. In fact, the major source of common dissatisfaction centered on death itself: those who had died young, like Stanley, talked constantly about plans gone awry, ambitions unfulfilled, children's lives still not set; those who had died old wailed about the miseries of age, the pain and indignity of long decline.

The truth, after all, was that little had changed. He had expected to have so much answered by now, either in the darkness of the void or in the light of eternity. Instead, it was dusk again, a lazy summer evening. Yet that, Stanley already understood, was the ultimate good fortune. The quest was not over. He had been spared once again, spared the end of doubt, preserved from eternal rest. Life, in other words, went on. With this discovery, Stanley found himself back in his accustomed place on the porch. He had often thought, as he sat in his old chair, that he could remain there for days; now, perhaps, he would be there forever. Raymond Street was quiet, the houses firm and solid in a line, under a gracious rain falling lightly onto a resting land.

In a Father's Place

DAN HAD FALLEN ASLEEP waiting for Nick and this Patty Keith, fallen deep into the lapping rhythm of a muggy Chesapeake evening, and when he heard the slam of car doors the sound came first from a dream. In the hushed amber light of the foyer Dan offered Nick a dazed and disoriented father's hug. Crickets seemed to have come in with them out of the silken night, the trill of crickets and honeysuckle pollen sharp as ammonia. Dan finally asked about the trip down, and Nick answered that the heat in New York had forced whole families onto mattresses in the streets. It looked like New Delhi, he said. Then they turned to meet Patty. She stood there in her Bermuda shorts and shirt, her brown hair in a bun, smelling of sweat and powder, and looking impatient. She fixed Dan in her eyes as she shook his hand, and she said, I'm so glad to meet *you*. Maybe she was just talking about the father of her boyfriend, and maybe no new lover ever walked into fair ground in this house, but Dan could not help thinking Patty meant the steward of this family's ground, the signer of the will.

"Nick has told me so much about this place," she said. Her look ran up the winding Georgian staircase, counted off the low, wide doorways, took note of a single ball-and-claw leg visible in the dining room, and rested on the highboy.

"Yes," said Dan. "It's marvelous." He could claim no personal credit for what Patty saw, no collector's eye, not even a decorator's hand.

Rachel had arrived from Wilmington earlier in the evening, and she appeared on the landing in her night-gown. She looked especially large up there after Dan had been fixed on Patty's compact, tight features; Rachel was a big girl, once a lacrosse defenseman. "Hey, honey," she yelled. There had been no other greeting for her younger brother since they were teen-agers. Nick returned a rather subdued hello. Tired, thought Dan, he's tired from the trip and he's got this girl to think about. Rachel came down the stairs; Patty took her hand with the awkwardness young women often show when shaking hands with other young women, or was it, Dan wondered as he watched these children meet in the breathless hall, a kind of guardedness?

Dan said, "You'll be on the third floor." He remem-bered his own father standing in the very place, saying these same words to polite, tired girls; he remembered the underarms and collar of his father's starched shirt, yellowed and brushed with salt. But it was different now: when Dan offered the third floor—and he had done so for some years now—he meant that Rachel or Nick could arrange themselves and their dates in the three bedrooms however they wished.

"The third floor?" said Patty. "Isn't your room on the second floor looking out on the water?" She appealed to Nick with her eyes.

"Actually, Dad," he said.

Dan was still not alert enough to handle conversation, especially this response that came from a place outside family tradition. "Of course," he said after a long pause. "Wherever you feel comfortable." She wants a room with a view, that's all, he cautioned himself. They had moved deeper into the hall, into a mildewed stillness that smelled of English linen and straw mats. They listened to the grandfather clock on the landing sounding eleven in an unhurried bass.

Dan turned to Patty. "It just means you'll have to share a bathroom with Ray, and she'll fight you to the last drop on earth."

But Patty did not respond to this attempt at charm, and fortunately did not notice Rachel's skeptical look. It was an old joke, or, at least, old for them. Dan remained standing in the hall, slowly recovering from his dense, inflamed sleep as Nick and Patty took their things to the room. Patty seemed pleased, in the end, with the arrangements, and after Dan had said good night and retired to his room, he heard them touring the house, stopping at the portrait of Edward, the reputed family ghost, and admiring the letters from General Washington in gratitude for service to the cause. Theirs wasn't a family of influence anymore, not even of social standing to those few who cared, but the artifacts in the house bracketed whole epochs in American history, with plenty of years and generations left over. He heard Patty saying Wow in her low but quite clear-timbred voice. Then he heard the door openings and closings, the run of toilets, a brief muffled conversation in the hall, and then a calm that returned the house to its creaks and groans, to sounds either real or imagined, a cry across the fields, the thud of a plastic trash can outside being knocked over by raccoons, the pulse of the tree toads, the hollow splash of rockfish and rays still feeding in the sleepless waters of the Bay.

A few years ago Dan had taken to saying that Rachel and Nick were his best friends, and even if he saw Nick rarely these days, he hoped it was largely the truth. He'd married young enough never to learn the art of adult friendship, and then Helen had died young enough for it to seem fate, though it was just a hit-and-run on the main street of Easton. Lucille Jackson had raised the kids. Since Helen died there had been three or four women in his life, depending on whether he counted the first, women he'd known all his life who had become free again one by one, girls he'd grown up with and had then discovered as he masturbated in his teens, or who had appeared with their young husbands at lawn parties in sheer cotton sundresses that heedlessly brushed those young thighs, or who now sat alone and distracted on bleachers in a biting fall wind and watched their sons play football. At some point Dan realized that if you stayed in a small town all your life, you could end up making love with every woman you had ever known and truly desired. Sheila Frederick had been there year after year in his dreams, at the lawn parties and football games, almost, it seemed to Dan later, as if she were stalking him through time. When they finally came together, Dan stepped freely into the fulfillment of his teenage fantasies, and then stood by almost helplessly as she ripped a jagged hole eight years wide out of the heart of his life. There had been one other woman since then, but it was almost as if he had lost his will, if not his lust; the first time he brought her to the house she asked him where he kept the soup bowls, and in that moment he could barely withstand the fatigue, the unbearable temptation to throw it all in, that this innocent question caused him.

He undressed in the heat and turned the fan to hit him squarely on the bed. The air it brought into the room was damp but no cooler, the fecund heat of greenhouses. He felt soft and pasty, flesh that had lost its tone, more spent than tired. He tried to remember if he had put a fan in Nick's room, knowing that Nick would not look for one but would blame him in the morning for the oversight; Rachel, in a similar place, would simply barge in and steal his. Dan knew better than to compare the two of them, and during adolescence boys and girls were incomparable anyway. But they were adults now, three years apart in their mid-twenties, and noticing their differences was something he did all the time. Rachel welcomed being judged among men; and her lovers, like the current Henry, were invariably cheerful, willing bores. This tough, assertive Patty Keith with those distrustful sharp eyes—there was something of Nick's other girls there, spiky, nursing some kind of damage, expecting fear. Patty would do better in the morning. They always did. But as he fell asleep finally, he was drifting back into history and memory, and it was not Patty Keith, and not even Helen meeting his father, but generations of young Eastern Shore women he saw, coming to this house to meet and be married, the ones who were pretty and eager for sex, the ones who were silent, the ones the parents loved much too soon, and the ones who broke their children's hearts.

In the morning Dan and Rachel ate breakfast together in the dining room, under the scrutiny of Cousin Oswald, who had last threatened his sinful parishioners in 1681. The portraitist had caught a thoroughly unpleasant scowl, a look the family had often compared to Lucille on off days. She had prepared a full meal with eggs, fried green tomatoes, and grits, a service reserved as a reward when they were all in the house. When Nick and the new girl did not come down, Lucille cleared their places so roughly that Dan was afraid she would chip the china.

"I'm done with mothering," she said, when Dan asked if she wasn't curious to meet Patty.

Dan and Rachel looked at each other and held their breath.

"I got six of my own to think about," she said. And then, as she had done for years, a kind of rebuke when Nick and Rachel were fighting or generally disobeying her iron commands, she listed their names in a single word. "LonFredMaryHennyTykeDerek."

"And you'd have six more if you could, besides Nick and me," said Rachel.

"And you better get started, *Miss* Rachel," she said.

"How about a walk," said Dan quickly.

August weather had settled in like a member of the family, part of the week's plans. The thick haze lowered a scorching dust onto the trees and fields, a blanched air that made the open pastures pitiless for the black Holsteins, each of them solitary in the heat except for the white specks of cowbirds perched on their withers. Dan was following Rachel down a narrow alley of brittle, dried-out box bushes. She was wearing a short Mexican shift and her legs looked just as solid now as they had when she cut upfield in her Princeton tunic. He would not call her manly, because hers was a big female form in the most classic sense, but he could understand that colleagues and clients, predominantly men, would find her unthreatening. She gave off no impression that she was prone to periodic weaknesses; they could count on her stamina, which, the older he got, Dan recognized as the single key to business. Nick was slight and not very athletic, just like Helen.

"So what do you think?" she asked over her shoulder.

"If you're talking about Patty I'm not going to answer. I don't think anything."

She gave him an uncompromising shrug.

They came out of the box bush on the lower lawn at the edge of the water and stood side by side. "The truth is," said Dan, "what I'm thinking about these days is Nick. I think I've made a hash of Nick."

"That's ridiculous." She stooped to pick a four-leaf clover out of an expanse of grass; she could do the same with arrowheads on the beach. They stood silently for a moment, looking at the sailboat resting slack on its mooring. It was a heavy boat, a nineteen-foot fiberglass sloop with a high bow, which Dan had bought after a winter's deliberation, balancing safety and speed the way a father must. When it arrived Nick hadn't even bothered to be polite. He wanted a "racing machine," something slender and unforgiving and not another "beamy scow." He was maybe ten at the time, old enough to know he could charm or hurt anytime he chose. Rachel didn't care much one way or the other—life was all horses for her—and Dan was so disappointed and angry with them both that he went behind the toolshed and wept.

"It's not. I really don't communicate with him at all. I don't even know what his book is about. Do you?"

"Well, I guess what it's really about is you. Not really you, but a father, and this place."

"Just what I was afraid of," said Dan.

"I don't think any of it will hurt your feelings, at least not the pieces I've read."

"Stop being so reassuring. A kiss-and-tell is not my idea of family fun." But Dan was already primed to be hurt. He'd been to a cocktail party recently where a woman he hardly knew forced him to read a letter from her daughter. It was a kind of retold family history, shaped by contempt, a letter filled with the word "never." This woman was not alone. It seemed so many of the people he knew were just now learning that their children would never forgive things, momentary failures of affection and pride, mistakes made in the barren ground between trying to keep hands off and the sin of intruding too much, things that seemed so trivial compared to a parent's embracing love. And even at the time Dan had never been sure what kind of father Nick wanted, what kind of man Nick needed in his life. Instead, Dan remembered confusion, such as the telephone calls he made when he still traveled, before Helen died. Rachel came to the phone terse and quick—she really was a kind of disagreeable girl, but so easy to read. Nick never had the gift of summarizing; his earnest tales of friends and school went on and on, until Dan, tired, sitting in a hotel room in Chicago, could not help but drop his coaxing nurturing tone and urge him to wrap it up. Too often, in those few short years, calls with Nick ended with the agreement that they'd talk about it more when he got home, which they rarely did.

"But that's really my point," said Dan after Rachel found nothing truly reassuring to say. "This has been going on for quite a while. I'm losing him. Maybe since your mother died, for all I know."

"Oh, give him time."

"He's changed. You can't deny that. He's lost the joy."

"No one wants to go through life grinning for everyone. It's like being a greeter in Atlantic City."

"I don't think he would have come at all this week if you weren't here." It felt good to say these things, even if he knew Rachel was about to tell him to stop feeling sorry for himself.

But Rachel cleared her throat, just the way her mother had when she had something important to say. "See," she said, "that's the thing. I've been waiting to tell you. I've got a job offer from a firm in Seattle, and I think I'm going to take it."

Dan stopped dead; the locusts were buzzing overhead like taut wires through the treetops. "What?"

"It's really a better job for me. It's general corporate practice, not just contracts."

"But you'll have to start all over again," he whined. "I'd really hate to see you go so far away."

"Well, that's the tough part."

Dan nodded, still standing in his footsteps. "I keep thinking, She can't do this, she's a girl. I'm sorry."

He forced himself to resume walking, and then to continue the conversation with the right kinds of questions—the new firm, how many attorneys, prospects for making partner—the questions of a father who has taught his children to live their own lives. They didn't touch on why she wanted to go to Seattle; three thousand miles seemed its own reason for the move, to be taken well or badly, just like Nick's novel. Dan pictured Seattle as a wholesome and athletic place, as if the business community all left work on Fridays in canoes across Puget Sound. It sounded right for Rachel. They kept walking up toward the stable, and Dan hung back while Rachel went in for a peek at a loved, but now empty, place. When she came back she stood before him and gave him a long hug.

"I'm sorry, but you'll have to humor the old guy," he said.

She did her best; Dan and Lucille had raised a kind woman. But there was nothing further to say and they continued the wide arc along the hayfield fences heavy with honeysuckle and back out onto the white road paved with oyster shells. They approached the house from the land side, past the old toolsheds and outbuildings, and Dan suddenly remembered the time Rachel was ten, when they were taking down storm windows and she had insisted on carrying them around for storage in the chicken coop. He was up on the ladder and heard a shattering of glass, and jumped from too high to find her covered in blood. Dr. Stout pulled the shards from her head without permanent damage or visible scar before turning to Dan's ankle, which was broken. Helen was furious. But the next time Dan had seen Dr. Stout was in the emergency room at Easton Hospital, and they were both covered with Helen's blood, and she was dead.

Patty had come down while they were gone, and Dan found her alone on the screened porch that had been once, and was still called, "the summer kitchen." It was open on three sides, separated from the old smokehouse on the far end by a small open space where Raymond, Lucille's old uncle, used to slaughter chickens and ducks. The yellow brick floor was hollowed by cooks' feet where the chimney and hearth had been; Dan could imagine the heat even in this broad, airy place. Patty was sitting on a wicker chair with her legs curled under her, wearing a man's strap undershirt and blue jogging shorts. She was reading a book, held so high that he could not fail to notice that it was by Jacques Derrida, a critic of some sort whose name Dan had begun to notice in the Sunday *New York Times*. Perhaps she had really not heard his approach, because she put the book down sharply when he called a good morning.

"Actually we've been up for hours," she said.

"Ah. Where's Nick?"

"He's working," she said with a protective edge on it.

Again, all Dan could find to say was "Ah." She smiled obscurely—her smiles, he observed, seemed to be directed inward—and he stood for a few more seconds before asking her if she would like anything from the kitchen. There was no question in his mind now: he was going to have to work with this one.

Rachel had just broken her news to Lucille, and the wiry, brusque lady who was "done with mothering" at breakfast was crying soundlessly into a paper towel.

"I don't know what it is about you children, moving so far away," she said finally. Dan knew at least one of her sons had moved to Salisbury, and she had daughters who had married and had gone even farther.

"We've gotten by, by ourselves," said Dan.

"But that was just for schooling, for training," she answered, training, if Dan understood her right, for coming back and assuming their proper places in the family tethers. She was leaning against the sink, a vantage point on her terrain, like Dan's desk chair, the places where both of them were putting in their allotted time. Rachel was sitting on the kitchen table, and she stayed there, much as she might have liked to come closer to Lucille and reach out to her.

Dan went back to the summer kitchen and sat beside the girl. "You'll have to excuse us. Rachel's just dropped a bit of a bombshell and we're all a little shaky."

"You mean about her moving to Seattle."

"Well, yes. That's right." He waited for her to offer some kind of vague sympathies, but she did not; it was asking too much of a young person to understand how much this news hurt.

"So," he said finally, "I hope you're comfortable here."

At this she brightened noticeably and put her book face down on the table. "It's a museum! Nick was going to set up his computer on that piecrust tea table. Can you imagine?"

Dan could picture it well, and he supposed it would be no worse than the time Nick had ascended the highboy, climbing from pull to pull, leaving deep sneaker scuffs on the mahogany burl as he struggled for purchase. But she was right, of course, and she had known enough to notice and identify a piecrust table. "You know antiques, then?"

Yes, she said, her mother was a corporate art consultant and her father, as long as Dan had asked, was a doctor who lived on the West Coast. She mentioned a few more pieces of furniture that had caught her eye.

"My mother thinks Chippendale and Queen Anne have peaked, maybe for a long time."

"I wouldn't know," said Dan.

"But the graveyard!" she exclaimed at the end.

Dan was relieved that she had finally listed something of no monetary value, peak or valley, something that couldn't be sold by her mother to Exxon. "As they say in town," he answered, "when most people die they go to heaven; if you're a Williams you just walk across the lawn."

"That's funny."

"I guess," he said. It was all of it crap, he reflected,

if he became the generation that lost its children. He'd be just as dead now as later.

"They're the essential past."

Essential past? Whatever could she mean, with her Derrida at her side, her antiques? "I'm not sure I understand what you mean, but to tell you the truth," he said, "I often think the greatest gift I could bestow on the kids is to bulldoze the place and relieve them of the burden."

"I think that's something for the two of them to decide."

"I suppose coming to terms with all this is what Nick is up to in his novel." The girl had begun to annoy him terribly and he could not resist this statement, even as he regretted opening himself to her answer.

"Oh," she said coyly, "I wouldn't say 'coming to terms.' No, I think just looking at it more reflectively. He's trying to deconstruct this family."

"Deconstruct? You mean destroy?" he said quickly, trying not to sound genuinely alarmed.

Patty gave him a patronizing look. "No. It's a critical term. It's very complicated."

Fortunately Nick walked in on this last line. It was Dan's first chance to get a look at him and he saw the full enthusiasm—and the smug satisfaction—of one who has worked a long morning while others took aimless walks. Nick was gangly, he would always be, even if he gained weight, but surprisingly quick. As unathletic as he was, he had been the kind of kid who could master inconsequential games of dexterity; he once hit a Paddle Pong ball a thousand times without missing, and could balance on a teeter-totter until he quit out of boredom. All his gestures, even his expressions, came on like compressed air. And while Dan had to work not to speculate on what part of himself had been "deconstructed" today, this tall, pacing, energetic man was the boy he treasured in his heart.

"The squire has been surveying the grounds?" said Nick.

"Someone has to work for a living," said Dan.

"I was wondering what you called it," he answered.

Patty watched this exchange with a confused look. Any kind of humor, even very bad humor, seemed utterly to escape her. "Did you finish the chapter?" she asked.

"No, but I broke through. I'm just a scene away. Maybe two."

"Well," she said with a deliberate pause, "wasn't that what you said yesterday?"

Good God, thought Dan, the girl wants to marry a published novelist, a novelist with antiques. He said quickly, "But it seems you had a great"—too much accent on the "great"—"a really very productive morning of work."

Nick's face darkened slightly, as fine a change as a razor cut. "It's kind of a crucial chapter. It has to be right."

"Were you tired?" she asked.

"No. It's just slow, that's all."

Rachel shouted down that lunch was ready, and Dan hung back for the kids to go first, and repeated this short conversation to himself. It was not such a large moment, he reflected, but nervous-making just the same, and during lunch Nick sat quietly while Patty filled the air with questions, questions about the family, about Lord Baltimore and the Calverts. They took turns answering her questions, but finally it fell to Nick to unlace the strands of the family, to place ancestors prominently at the Battle of Yorktown. He looked now and again to Dan for confirmation, and Dan knew how he felt reciting these facts that, even if true, could only sound like family puffery. Dan wanted to do better by his son and did try to engage himself in the conversation, but by the time Lucille had cleared the plates he felt full of despair, gummy with some kind of sadness for all of them, for himself, for Rachel now off to Seattle in a place where maybe no one would marry her, for Nick with this girl, for Lucille so much older than she looked and hiding, Dan knew it, her husband's bad health from everyone.

Patty ended the meal by offering flatteries all around the table, including compliments to Lucille that sent her back to the kitchen angrily—but loud enough only for Dan's practiced ear—mimicking the girl's awkward phrase, "So pleasant to have eaten such a good lunch." As they left the table finally, Dan announced he had to spend the afternoon in his office. At this point, he wasn't sure what he would less rather do. He changed quickly and left for town with the three of them in the summer kitchen discussing the afternoon, and he could hear Rachel laboring for every word.

He was so distracted as he drove to town that he nearly ran the single stoplight. Driving mistakes of any kind went right to his living memory; once he rear-ended a car slightly on Route 301, and he bolted to the bushes and threw up in front of the kids, in front of a very startled carload of hunters. He crawled to Lawyers' Row and came in the door pale enough for Mrs. Victor—it had always been *Mrs.* Victor—to comment on the heat and ask him if his car air conditioner was working properly. His client was waiting for him, Bobbie Perlee, one of those heavy, fleshy teenagers in Gimme caps and net football jerseys with greasy long hair. The smell of frying oil and cigarettes filled his office. Whenever he had thought of Rachel joining his practice, he had reminded himself that she would spend her time with clients like this one, court-appointed, Bobbie Perlee in trouble with the law again for assaulting his friend Aldene McSwain with a broken fishing pole. McSwain could lose the eye yet. But Dan couldn't blame a thousand Perlees on anyone but himself; he had made the choice when it became clear that the kids needed him closer to home and not working late night after night across the Bay in Washington. If she had lived, Helen would have insisted on it anyway.

"What do you have to say this time, Bobbie?"

Bobbie responded with the round, twangy O's of the Eastern Shore, a sound that for so long had spelled ignorance to Dan, living here on a parallel track. He said nothing in response to Bobbie's description of the events; he didn't really hear them. Bobbie Perlee pawed his fat feet into Dan's worn-out Persian rug. For a moment it all seemed so accidental to Dan; sitting in this office with the likes of Bobbie Perlee seemed both frighteningly new and endlessly rehearsed. He could only barely remember the time when escape from the Eastern Shore had given meaning to and guided everything he did. It was there when he refused to play with the Baileys and Pacas, children of family and history like himself. It was there when he refused to go to "the University," which, in the case of Maryland gentry, meant the University of Pennsylvania. It was there even the night he first made love, because it was with his childhood playmate, Dorsey Tobin. They had escaped north side by side for college, and came together out of loneliness, and went to bed as if breaking her hymen would shatter the last ring that circled them both on these monotonous farmlands and tepid waters.

But he'd come back anyway when his father was dying, and brought Helen with him, a Jew and a Midwesterner who came with a sense of discovery, a fresh eye on the landscape. Helen had given the land back to Dan before she was gone. Then Sheila Frederick came back out of his youth like a lost bookend, with a phone call saying, *I don't look the same, you know,* and because none of them did—it had been thirty years—it meant she was still pretty. She lived now in a bright new rivershore condo in Chestertown. She *was* still pretty, but now, when she relaxed, her mouth settled into a tight line of bitterness. Their last night, two years ago, after a year of fighting, she told Dan she worried about his aloneness, not his loneliness, which was, she said, her problem and a female one at that, but his aloneness as he rattled around that huge house day after day, with no company but that harsh and unforgiving Lucille. From her, this talk and pre-diction of a solitary life was a threat; to Dan, at that moment anyway, being alone was perfect freedom.

Dan finally waved Perlee out of his office without anything further said. These lugs, he could move them around like furniture and they'd never ask why. Dan looked out his office window onto the Queen Anne's County courthouse park, a cross-hatching of herring-bone brick pathways shaded under the broad leaves of the tulip trees. At the center gathering of the walks was a statue of Queen Anne that had been rededi-cated by Princess Anne herself. She was only a girl at the time but could have told that wildly enthusiastic crowd a thing or two about history, if they'd chosen to listen. Dan had done well by his children, if today was any indication. They were free, not because they had to be, but because they wanted to be. Rachel won a job offer from three thousand miles away because she was that good. My God, how would he bear it when she was gone? And Nick was reaching adulthood with a passion, on the wings of some crazy notion about literary deconstruction that—who knew?—could well be what they all needed to hear and understand. So, in many ways, his thoughts ended with this sad girl, this Patty Keith, who seemed the single part of his life that didn't have to be, yet it was she who had been tugging him into depression and ruminations on the bondages of family and place all afternoon.

On the way home he stopped at Mitchell Brothers liquors, a large windowless block building with a sign on the side made of a giant S that formed the first letter of "SPIRITS, SUBS, AND SHELLS"; the shells, of course, were the kind you put into shotguns and deer rifles. The Mitchells were clients of his and were very possibly the richest family in town. He bought a large bottle of Soave and at the last minute added a jug of Beefeater's, which was unusual enough for Doris Mitchell to ask if he was having a party. He answered that Nick was home with a girlfriend that looked like trouble and he was planning to drink the gin himself.

The summer kitchen was empty when he stepped out, gin-and-tonic in hand. A shower and a first drink had helped. He might have hoped for the three of them, now fully relaxed, to be there trading stories, but instead they came out one by one, and everyone was carrying something to read. He supposed Patty was judging him for staring out at the trees and water, no obscure Eastern European novel in his hand. Nick was uncommunicative, sullen really, sullenness in the place of the sparkling joy he used to bring into the house. Dinner passed quickly. Afterward, Patty insisted that Nick take her to the dock and show her the stars and the lights of Kent Island the way, she said firmly, he'd *promised* he would. Rachel and Dan turned in before they got back and Dan read *Newsweek* absently until the last of the doors had closed, and he slipped out of his room for one of his house checks, the changing of the guard from the mortals of evening to the ghosts of the midwatch. He was coming back to his room when he heard a cry from Nick's room. In shame and panic he realized immediately that they were making love, but before he could flee he heard her say "No. No." It wasn't that she was being forced, he could tell that immediately; instead, there was a harshness to it that, even as a father is repelled at the idea of listening to his son have sex, forced Dan to remain there. He had not taken a breath, had not shifted his weight off the ball of his left foot; if anyone had come to the door he would not have been able to move. There was more shuffling from inside, a creak as they repositioned in the old sleigh bed. *"That's* right," said Patty finally, "like *that.* Like that." Her voice, at least, was softer now, clouded by the dreaminess of approaching orgasm. "Like that," she breathed one last time, and came with a heave. But from Nick, this whole time, there had not been a word, not a grunt or a sound, so silent he was that he might not have been there at all.

"I think she's a witch," said Rachel. They were on their post-breakfast walk again, this time both of them digging in their heels in purposeful strides.

Dan let out a disgusted and fearful sigh.

"No. I mean it. I think she's using witchcraft on him."

"If you'll forgive the statement, it's cuntcraft if it's anything."

"That's pretty, Dad," she said. They had already reached the water and were turning into the mowed field. "But I'm telling you, it was spooky."

All night Dan had pictured Patty coming, her legs tight around Nick's body, her thin lips clenched pale, and her white teeth dripping blood.

"She controls him. She tells him what to do," said Rachel. "If this were Salem she'd be swinging as we speak."

They had now walked along the hayfield fence line through the brown grass, and said nothing more as they turned for the house, its lime-brushed brick soft and golden in the early-morning sun.

"It won't last. He'll get over her," he said.

"Yes, but the older you are, the longer it takes to grow out of things, wouldn't you say?"

Dan nodded; Rachel, as usual, was quite right about that. It had taken him six months to figure out that Sheila Frederick was one of the worst mistakes of his life, and another seven years to do something about it. It would not have been so bad if it weren't for the kids. He could admit and confess almost everything in his life except for the fact that he had known, for years, how much they hated her. They hated her so much that, when it was over, Nick didn't even bother to comment except to tell Dan he'd seen her twice slipping family teaspoons into her purse.

They skirted the graveyard and without discussion bypassed the house for another tour. As they went by, Dan glanced over his shoulder, and there she was, Derrida in hand, a small voracious lump that had taken over a corner of the summer kitchen. He looked up at the open window where Nick was working.

"I think I'd better marry Henry," said Rachel.

"He's a very nice guy. You know how fond of him I am," said Dan.

"Nice, but not very interesting. Is that what you mean?"

"Not at all. But as long as you put it that way, I think this Patty Keith is interesting."

"So what are we going to do about Miss Patty?" asked Rachel.

"Well, nothing. What can we do? Nick's already mad at me; I'm not going to give him reason to hate me by butting into his relationships."

"But here's the problem. Someday Nick's going to wake up—but maybe not for a year, or ten years—and he'll realize he's just given years of his life to that witch, and then isn't he going to wonder where his sister and father were all that time?"

"It doesn't work that way. Believe me. You don't blame your mistakes in love on others."

Rachel turned to look at him fully with just the slightest narrowing of focus. It was an expression any lawyer, from the first client meeting to the last summary to the jury, had to possess. "Are you talking about Mrs. Frederick?" she said finally.

"I suppose I am. I'm not saying others don't blame you for the mistakes you make in love." Without any trouble, without even a search in his memory, Dan could list several things Sheila had made him do that the kids should never, ever forgive.

"No one blames you for her. The cunt."

Dan was certain that Rachel had never before in her whole life used that word. He laughed, and so did Rachel, and he put his arm around her shoulder for a few steps.

She said finally, with an air of summary, "I really think you're making a mistake. I believe she's programming him. I mean it. I think she's dangerous to him and to us. It happens to people a lot more resilient and less sensitive than Nick."

"We'll see." They walked for a few more minutes, in air that was so still that the motion of their steps felt like relief. Again Rachel was right; he was a less sensitive man than his son, but he had been equally powerless to resist the eight years he had spent with Sheila. Dan couldn't answer for his own life, much less Nick's, so they completed their dejected morning walk and climbed the brick steps to the back portico. As they reached the landing, he took his daughter in his arms again and said, "God, Rachel, I'm going to miss you."

When they came back, Patty was in the kitchen talking to Lucille. From the sound of it she had been probing for details about Nick as a boy, which could have been a lovely scene if it hadn't been Patty, eyes sharp, brain calculating every monosyllabic response, as if, in the middle of it, she might take issue with Lucille and start correcting her memories. It's not the girl's fault, thought Dan; it's just a look, the way her face moves, something physical. There was no way for Patty to succeed with Lucille; no girl of Nick's could have done better. It's not Patty's fault, Dan said to himself; she's trying to be nice, but she just doesn't have any manners; her parents haven't given her any grace. He said this to himself again later in the morning when she poked her head into his study and asked if his collection of miniature books was valuable. Mother obviously did not deal in miniatures, although, Dan supposed, she would be eager to sell Audubons to IBM. Dan answered back truthfully that he didn't know, some of his books might be valuable, as a complete collection it could be of interest to someone. She took this information back with her to the summer kitchen. Dan watched her walk down the hall in a short sweatshirt that exposed the hollow of her back and a pair of tight jersey pants that made her young body look solid as a brick.

Dan did not see Nick come down, did not hear whether he had finished his chapter and whether that was enough for Patty. At lunch Rachel noted that the Orioles were playing a day game, and Dan had to remind himself again that, except for sailing, the athlete in the family was the girl, that she'd been not only older but much more physical than her brother. He remembered how he and Helen had despaired about Nick, a clinger, quick to burst into tears at the first furrowing of disapproval; how Dan had many times caught a tone from the voices in the school playground across the street from his office, and how he had often stopped to figure out if it was Nick's wail he heard or just the high-pitched squeals of the girls, or the screech of tires on some distant street. And how curious it was that with this softness also came irrepressible energy, the force of the family, as if he saved every idea and every flight of joy for Dan and Rachel. Yet it had been years now since Nick had turned it on for him.

For once, Patty seemed content to sit at the sidelines, while Rachel and Nick continued with the Orioles. Name the four twenty-game winners in 1971, asked Rachel, and Nick, of course, could manage only the obvious one, Jim Palmer. Rachel's manners—they were Lucille's doing as much as his, Dan reminded himself—compelled her to ask Patty if she could do any better; Patty made a disgusted look and went back to her crab salad. At that point Dan saw the chance he had been waiting for, and he turned to Nick and told him he had to go to see a client's boat—a Hinckley 41—that had been rammed by a drunk at Chestertown mooring. "Come on along and we'll catch up," he said offhandedly. He looked straight into Nick's eyes and would not allow him to glance toward Patty.

"Hey great," said Nick after the slightest pause. "How about later in the afternoon?"

"Nope. Got to go at low tide. The boat sank." His tone was jocular, the right one for cornering his son before Patty could move, before she started to break into the conversation with her "Wait a minute" and her "I don't understand." Rachel moved fast as well and quickly suggested, in a similar tone, that they, in the meantime, would go see the Wye oak, the natural wonder of the Eastern Shore. "We can buy T-shirts," said Rachel.

"But—"

A few minutes later Dan and Nick were on the road in Dan's large Oldsmobile. There was considerable distance between them on the seat. "I hope Patty doesn't mind me stealing you like this," Dan said finally.

Nick could not hide his discomfort, but he waved it off.

"Women," said Dan.

Nick let out a small laugh. He was sitting with his body turned slightly toward the door, gazing out at the familiar sights, the long sheds of Lansdale's chicken operation, the rustic buildings of the 4-H park under the cool shade of tall loblolly pines.

"So how's it going? The novel."

Good, he said. He'd finished his chapter.

"You know," said Dan, working up to something he'd planned to say, "I'm interested to read it anytime you're ready to show it. I won't mention it again, just so long as you know. I can't wait to see what it's about."

"Oh," said Nick, "it's not really *about* anything, not a plot anyway. I'm more interested in process. It's kind of part of a critical methodology."

Dan wanted to ask what in the world that meant, but could not. "Patty seems interested. I'm sure that's helpful."

"Patty's energy," Nick said, finally turning straight on the seat, "is behind every word."

"She certainly is a forceful girl." Dan realized his heart was pounding, and that it was breaking as he watched Nick come to life at the mention of her name.

"She tore the English Department at Columbia *apart*." He laughed at some private memory that Dan really did not want to hear. "I know she's not for everyone, but I've never known anyone who takes less shit in her life."

And I love her, he was saying. I'm in love with her because she doesn't take shit from anyone. Not like you, Dan heard him think, living out your life a prisoner of family history. Not like you, who let Mrs. Frederick lock me out the night I ran away from my finals freshman year. Dan supposed the list was endless.

And at this impasse something could well have ended for him and Nick. It would not come as a break, a quarrel, but it would also not come unexpectedly or undeservedly. In the end, thought Dan, being Nick's father didn't mean he and his son couldn't grow apart;

didn't mean a biological accident gave him any power over the situation. It only meant that it would hurt more. He could not imagine grieving over friends he once loved with all his heart and now never saw. The Hellmans, how he had loved them, and where in the world were they now? But Nick—even if he never spoke to him again, even if this Patty Keith took him away to some isolation of spirit, Dan would know where he was and feel the pain.

"So why so glum, Dad?" said Nick, a voice very far away from the place where Dan was lost in thought.

"What?"

"I mean, we're going to see a wreck, a Hinckley, for Christ's sake, and you're acting like you owned it yourself."

They were crossing the long bridge over the Chester, lined, as always, with market fishermen sitting beside plastic pails of bait and tending three or four poles apiece. Twenty years ago they'd all been black, now they were mostly white, but there had not been too much other change in this seventeenth-century town; Dan had never known how to take this place, old families preserving everything to the last brick even as they washed and sloshed their way down Washington Street on rivers of gin. But it was a lovely town, rising off the river on the backsides of gracious houses, brick and slate, with sleeping porches resting out over the tulip trees in a line of brilliant white slats. Dan looked ahead at this pleasant scene while Nick craned his neck out to the moorings.

"Oh yes," he said. "There's a mast at a rather peculiar angle."

The boat was a mess, lying on its side on a sandbar in a confused struggle of lines, a tremendous fibrous gash opening an almost indecent view of the forward berths. Nick rowed them out in a dingy; he was full of cheer, free, no matter what, on the water. The brown sandbar came up under them at the edge of the mooring like a slowly breaching whale. As they came alongside, Nick jumped out and waded over to the boat, poked his head through the jagged scar, and then started hooting with laughter.

"What is it?" said Dan.

Nick backed his head out of the hull. "Porn videos. God, there must be fifty of them scattered over the deck."

Dan quickly flashed a picture of his rather proper Philadelphia client, who could have no idea that his most secret compartment had burst in the crash.

"Jesus," said Nick. "Here's one that is actually called *Nick My Dick*. It's all-male."

"Stop it. It's none of your business," said Dan, but he could not help beaming widely as he said this, and together they plowed the long way back through the moorings, making loud and obnoxious comments about most of the boats they passed. Dan doubted that any of these tasteless, coarse stinkpots, all of the new ones featuring a dreadful palette of purples and plums, contained a secret library to compare with the elegant white Hinckley's. After they returned the boat, they strolled up Washington Street to the court square and stopped for an ice cream at one of the several new "quality" establishments that had begun to spring up here. Dan hoped, prayed, only that Sheila Frederick, who lived here, would not choose this moment to walk by, but if she did she would simply ignore him anyway, which would not be a bad thing for Nick to see.

But it was all circumscribed by the return, as if Nick were on furlough. And it was certain to be bad; Dan could sense it by now as they turned through the gates back to the farm. This time, when they reentered the summer kitchen, the Derrida remained raised. As far as Dan could tell, she had made little headway in this book, but she stuck to it through Nick's stray, probing comments about their trip. For the first time she struck Dan as funny, touchingly adolescent, with her tight little frown and this pout that she seemed helpless, like a twelve-year-old, to control. No, she had *not* gone to see the Wye oak. No, she did not wish for any iced tea.

This is how it went for the rest of the day and into the evening. She's in quite a snit, said Rachel when they passed in the front hall, both of them pretending not to be tiptoeing out of range of the summer kitchen, which had seemed to grow large and overpowering around that hard nub of rage. Nick also circled, spending some of the time reading alongside the girl, some of the time upstairs writing, perhaps, a whole new chapter, a whole new volume, as penance. It was Lucille's day off, and normally eating at the kitchen table gave the family leave to loosen up, a kind of relief from the strictures of this life. Patty sat but did not eat, just made sure that everyone understood, as Nick might have said, that she wouldn't take this shit. Dan could not imagine what she was telling herself, how she had reconstructed the events of the afternoon to give her sufficient reason for all this. In the silence, everything in the kitchen, the pots and pans, the appliances and spices, all this unnecessary clutter, seemed to close in. The pork chops tasted like sand; the back of the chair cut into his spine. He tried to picture how she might describe this to friends, if she had any. He could not guess which one of them had earned the highest place in this madness, but he knew which one of them would pay. He'd seen it in couples all his life, these cycles of offense and punishment, had lived the worst of it himself with Sheila Frederick. When she finally left the table and Nick followed a few minutes later—he gave a kind of shrug, but his face was blank—Rachel tried to make a slight joke of it. "We are displeased," she said.

"No. This is tragic," said Dan. "She's mad."

They cleaned the dishes, and after Rachel kissed him good night he went out into the darkness of the summer kitchen. The air, so still all day, was still motionless but was beginning to come alive; he could hear the muffled clang of the bell buoy a mile into the river. A break in the heat was coming; the wildlife that never stopped encroaching on this Chesapeake life always knew about the weather in advance, and their voices became shortened and sharp, their movements through the trees or across the lawns became quick dashes from cover to cover; they were ready, even to the last firefly, whose brief flashes gave only a staccato edginess to a darkening night. Dan felt old; he was tired. For a moment or two his unspoken words addressed the spirits of the house—they too never stopped encroaching—but he stopped abruptly because he knew, had known since he was a boy, that if he let them in he would never again be free of them. He wondered if Helen would be among them. He waited long enough, deep enough, into this skittish night, for everyone to be asleep; he could not stand the thought of hearing a single sound from Nick's room. But when he finally did turn in, he could not keep from hesitating for a moment at the door, much as he and Helen used to when the children were infants and needed only the sound of a moist breath to know all was well.

Under the door he saw the light was on, and through it he heard the low mumble of a monotone. It was she, and it was just a steady drone, a break now and again, a slightly higher inflection once or twice. It was a sheet of words, sentences, if they were written, that would swallow whole paragraphs, and though Dan wanted to think this unemotional tone meant her anger was spent, he knew immediately that this girl was abusing his son. She was interrogating him without questions; she was damning him without accusations, just this litany, an endless rosary of rage. It could well have been going on for hours, words from her mad depths replacing Nick's, supplanting his thoughts. He could make out no phrases except, once, for a distinct "What we're discussing here . . ." that was simply a pause in the process as she forced him to accept not only her answers but her questions as well. He did not know how long he stood there; he was waiting, he realized after a time, for the sound of Nick's voice, because as Dan swayed back and forth in the hall, he could imagine anything, even that she had killed him and was now incoherently continuing the battle over his body. When finally the voice of his son did appear, it was just two words: "Christ, Patty." There was only one way to read these two names: he was begging, pleading, praying for her to stop. And then the drone began again.

Dan closed his bedroom door carefully behind him, and sat by his bay window in an old wingback that had been Helen's sewing chair. Her dark mahogany sewing table was empty now, the orderly rows of needles and spooled threads scattered over the years. The wide windows beckoned him. He could feel no breezes on his sweating forehead and neck, but the air was flavored now with manure, milk, gasoline, and rotting silage, a single essence of the farm that was seeping in from the northwest on the feet of change. He stared out into the dark for a long time before he undressed, and was still half awake when the first blades of moving air began to slice through the humidity. He was nodding off on his pillow when, later, he heard the crustacean leaves of the magnolias and beeches begin to clatter in the wind.

The house was awakened by the steady blow, an extravagance of air and energy after these placid weeks of a hot August. Dan could hear excited yips from the kitchen, as if the children were teenagers once again; he thought, after what he had heard and the hallucinations that plagued him all night long, that he was dreaming an especially cruel vision of a family now lost. But he went down to the kitchen and they were all there: Rachel, as usual grumpy and slow-moving in the morning and today looking matronly and heavy in her long unornamented nightgown; Patty, standing on the other side by the refrigerator with a curiously unsure look; Lucille at her most abrupt, wry best; and Nick, wearing nothing but his bathing suit, pacing back and forth, filled with the joy and energy that only a few hours ago Dan had given up as lost forever.

"A real wind," he said. "A goddamn hurricane."

"Shut your mouth with that," said Lucille happily.

"We're going to sail all the way to the *bridge*," he continued, and poked Rachel in the side with a long wooden spoon until she snarled at him.

"I've got to wash my hair," said Rachel.

"Fuck your hair." Lucille grabbed her own wooden spoon and began to move toward him, and he backed off toward Patty, who was maybe tired out from her efforts of the night before, or maybe just so baffled by this unseen Nick that even she could not intrude. Nick picked her up by the waist and spun her around. She was still in her short nightgown, and when Nick grabbed, he hiked it over her underpants; even as Dan helplessly noticed how sexy her body was, he recoiled at the thought of Nick touching it. With mounting enthusiasm, Dan watched this nervy move and wondered whether it would work on her, but she struggled to get down and was clearly furious as she caught her footing.

"I agree with Rachel," she said. It was probably, Dan realized, the first time she'd ever used Rachel's name.

Nick persisted. "Wind like this happens once a year. It might blow out."

"It could be flat calm again by lunch," said Dan.

Patty turned quickly on Dan as if he hadn't the slightest right to give an opinion, to speak at all. "I *understand*," she whined. "I just think this is a good chance for him to get work done."

It was "him" Dan noticed. He waited for Nick's next move and almost shouted with triumph when it came.

"Fuck work." As he said this, a quite large honey-locust branch cracked off the tree outside the window and fell with a thud through a rustle of leaves.

Patty screwed her face into a new kind of scowl— she had more frowns, thought Dan, and scowls and pouts than any person he had ever met—and announced, "Well, I'm not going. I'm going to get *something* done."

"Derrida?" said Dan. He was still giddy with relief. She glared.

"Oh, come on, sweetie," Nick coaxed. "You won't believe what sailing in wind like this is like." He tried cajoling in other ways, promises of unbroken hours of work, a chance to see the place from the water; he even made public reference to the fight of the day before when he told her a sail would "clear the air after that awful night." He could be worn down by this, Dan knew; he could still lose. But earlier in the conversation Rachel had slipped out and now, with a crash of the door that was probably calculated and intentional, she came back into the kitchen in her bathing suit—she really should watch her weight, Dan couldn't avoid thinking—and that was all the encouragement Nick needed.

Dan walked down to the water with them and sat on the dock as they rigged the boat. The Dacron sails snapped in slicing folds; the boom clanked on the deck like a road sign flattened to the pavement in a gale. "Is it too much?" he called out. Of course it was; under normal circumstances he would be arguing strenuously that it was dangerous. They all knew it was too much. Nick called back something, but he was downwind and the sound was ripped away as soon as he opened his mouth. They cast off and in a second had been blown a hundred feet up the creek. They struggled quickly to haul in the sails; Rachel was on the tiller and Dan wished she wasn't, because she was nowhere near the sailor Nick was; she would have been better on the sheets where her brute strength could count. But she let the boat fall off carefully and surely, and all of a sudden the wind caught the sails with a hollow, dense thud, and as they powered past the dock upwind toward the mouth of the creek, Dan heard Nick yell, full voice and full of joy, "Holy shit!"

When he got back to the house she was in her place in the summer kitchen. How tired he was of her presence, of feeling her out there. All the time—it was maybe nothing more than a family joke, but it was true—she had been sitting in his chair. Nick might have told her, or she might have even sensed it. He walked through the house and was met, as he expected, as he had hoped, with an angry, hostile stare.

"You don't approve of water sports, I gather?" he said, ending curiously on a slightly British high point.

She fixed him with her slitty eyes; this was the master of the Columbia English Department.

"Not interested?" he asked again.

"As a matter of fact, I don't approve of very much around here."

"I'm sorry for that," he said. He still held open the possibility that the conversation could be friendly, but he would not lead it in that direction. "It hasn't seemed to have gone well for you."

"There's nothing wrong with *me*."

"Ah ha."

"I think you're all in a fantasy."

Dan made a show of looking around at the walls, the cane-and-wicker furniture, and ended by rapping his knuckles on the solid table. He shrugged. "People from the outside seem to make a lot more of this than we do," he said.

She leaned forward slightly, this was the master of his son. "It's not for me to say, but when you read Nick's novel you'll know where *he* stands."

The words exploded from him. "How dare you bring Nick's novel into this?"

"Why do you think he wanted to come here, anyway?"

"Patty," said Dan, almost frightened by the rage that was now fevering his muscles, "when it comes to families, I really think you should let people speak for themselves. I think you should reconsider this conversation."

"You have attacked me. You have been sarcastic to me. I have nothing to apologize for." She made a slight show of returning to her book.

"Tell me something. What are your plans? What are your plans for Nick?"

"Nick makes his own plans."

It was not a statement of fact; it was a threat, a show of her larger power over him. "And you? What are your plans?"

"I'm going to live my own life and I'm not going to pretend that all this family shit comes to anything."

"Whose family? Yours or Nick's?"

"You mean do I plan to marry Nick? So I can get my hands on this?" She mimicked his earlier gesture. "I suppose that's why from the second, the very second

I walked in, you have disapproved of me. Well, don't worry"—she said this with a patronizing tone, addressing a child, a pet—"the only thing I care about around here is Nick and—" She cut herself off.

"And what?"

"And his work. Not that it matters to you."

"Oh, cut the crap about his work. You want his soul, you little Nazi, you want any soul you can get your hands on."

She pounded the table with her small fist. "What we're talking about here," she shouted, and Dan's body recoiled with this phrase, "is the shit you have handed out, and I'll cite chapter and verse, and—"

"Patty, Patty." He interrupted her with difficulty. "Stop this."

"I have some power, you know."

"Patty, I think it would be better for everyone if you left. Right now."

"What?"

"You heard me."

"You would throw me out?" She did, finally, seem quite stunned. "And just what do you think Nick's going to do when he gets back?"

"I don't know. But I will not tolerate you in my house for another minute."

She slammed her feet down on the brick floor and jumped up almost as if she planned to attack him, to take a swing at him. "Okay. I'll go. I'm not going to take this shit."

She marched through the kitchen, and a moment

or two later he heard a door slam. He moved from his seat to his own chair; suddenly the view seemed right again, the pecan lined up with the blue spruce by the water, and the corner of the smokehouse opened onto a hay land that had, from this vantage, always reminded him of the fields of Flanders. A few minutes later he heard a heavy suitcase being dragged over the yellow pine staircase, the steel feet clanking like golf spikes over the Georgian treads. He heard a mumble as she came to the kitchen to say something tactical to Lucille, perhaps to give her a note for Nick or to play the part of the tearful girl unfairly accused. He heard the trunk of her car open and he pictured her hefting her large bag, packed with dresses and shortie nightgowns and diaphragms and makeup, over the lip of her BMW, and then she was off, coming into view at the last minute in a flash of red.

Dan heard Lucille's light step, and then saw her face peer out into the summer kitchen. As many times as Dan had tried to make her change, she never liked to come into a room to say something but would stand in the doorway and make everyone crane their necks to see her.

"Mr. Dan?"

"Lucille, *please* come out."

She took two steps. "You're in a mess of trouble now."

He held his arms up. "What could I do?"

"I got six of my own to worry about." She shrugged and then gave him one of her rare, precious smiles.

The wind was singing through the screens in a single, sustained high note. "But I do hope to the Good Lord that those babies are okay out in this storm."

Dan stayed in the summer kitchen all morning. The winds weren't going to die down this time—he knew that the moment he woke up—it was a storm with some power to it and it would bring rain later in the day. He ate lunch in his study, and around two went down to the dock. The water was black and the wind was slicing the wave tops into fine spray. No one should be out in this, and especially not his two children. He pictured them taking turns at the tiller as the boat pounded on the wave bottoms and broke through the peaks in a shattering of foam. He wasn't worried yet; he'd selected that big boat for days like this. It would swamp before it would capsize, and they could run for a sandy shore any time they wanted. The winds would send them back to this side; he'd sailed more than one submerged hulk home as a boy, and he'd left a boat or two on the beach and hiked home through the fields. This was the soul of the Chesapeake country, never far from land on the water, the water always meeting the land, always in flux. You could run from one to the other. The water was there, in the end, with Sheila, because he had triumphed over her, had fought battles for months in telephone calls that lasted for hours and evenings drowned in her liquor, until one morning he had awakened and listened to the songs from the water and realized that he was free.

He lowered his legs over the dock planking and sat

looking out into the Bay. From this spot, he had watched the loblolly pines on Carpenter's Island fall one by one across the low bank into the irresistible tides. When the last of the pines had gone, the island itself was next, and it sank finally out of sight during the hurricanes of the fifties. Across the creek Mr. McHugh's house stood empty, blindfolded by shutters. What was to become of the place now that the old man's will had scattered it among nieces and nephews? What was to happen to his own family ground if Rachel went to Seattle for good and Nick . . . and Nick left this afternoon never to come back?

Dan tried to think again of what he would say to Nick, what his expression should be as they closed upon the mooring, what his first words should cover. But the wind that had already brought change brushed him clean of all that and left him naked, a man. He could not help the rising tide of joy that was coming to him. He was astonished by what had happened to him. By his life. By the work he had done, the wills, the clients, all of them so distant that he couldn't re-member ever knowing them at all. By the wife he had loved, and lost on the main street of Easton, and by the women who had since then come in and out of his life, leaving marks and changes he'd never even both-ered to notice. By the children he had fathered and raised, those children looking out from photographs over mounds of Christmas wrappings and up from the water's edge, smiles undarkened even by their mother's death. By his mistakes and triumphs, from the slap of a doctor's hand to the last bored spadeful of earth. It was all his, it all accumulated back toward him, toward his body, part of a journey back through the flesh to the seed where it started, and would end.

Mary in the Mountains

SHE WROTE TO SAY THIS: *Send me a picture of the boy we never had, the one with blue eyes, big ears, and a smile that says, Nothing, so far, has hurt too bad.*

She wrote: *Yesterday, when I got your letter, I carried it with me like a dark bloom. I took it with me when I went swimming at the dam, and I lay down in the sun, gray-haired and white. A few feet away from me two high-school girls with long, thin bodies dove into the water without a ripple or splash. They wore black bathing suits stretched from hipbone to hipbone across their flat stomachs, and I touched your letter to make sure it was addressed to me.*

She wrote: *I think of you now when I look at the oak tree standing apart in the lower corner of my field. Last winter, against the snow, I saw your profile—it was your nose—in the branches. This summer there will be growth, and the deadwood that forms your eyebrows*

will not make it through the winter, but that is right:
you were always leaving anyway. When I look at that
tree, I think of you with your deep tangled roots and
your fresh buds, but mostly I think of you alone.

Mary rarely laughed; she was silent in groups and
was content to pass unnoticed by anyone but Will
through his boisterous college days; she stuttered,
often, on Ts and Ws. She and Will were married in
June 1958, in a white New Hampshire church with
high wooden trusses, under a cross made of spruce
that had twisted and checked. She wore her grandmother's dress, petticoats, and lace, but as she came
down the aisle it was her black hair and white skin
and green eyes that people noticed. Will mumbled,
but she repeated her vows so clearly and slowly, with
such conviction and determination, that husbands and
wives all through the congregation squirmed and
avoided each other's eyes.

Will's friends, a week out of college, were disappointed by the food, the lodging, Mary's bridesmaids,
the lack of liquor and late-night bars. Will had warned
them to expect little, just as he had tried to explain
Mary to them for the past two years. The ushers left
the quiet reception as soon as Mary and Will did, and
reconvened that night in Boston for a party they would
all remember for the rest of their lives. Years later Will
heard about it and it hurt his feelings.

Will's mother never warmed to Mary—she had recognized, as few others ever had, that Mary was a mouse

that wasn't afraid to show its teeth—but Will loved her so much he stayed awake at night counting the times she breathed.

They went to Europe for the Grand Tour. Will's mother told everyone at the reception that at least the honeymoon would be festive and gay, but they spent most of the first month in cathedrals. Will listened in the gloomy shadows as she explained the tympanum at Vézelay, the chancel at Chartres, the altar and relics of Rouen. He wore Bermuda shorts and black shoes and socks, a handsome face made featureless by his sandy crew cut and heavy black glasses. Even so, he worried what the Europeans would make of Mary in her plain cotton shifts and wide-brimmed straw hat, with her earnest look and stuttering French.

In their travels, they met, as planned, with three of his ushers making a tour of nightclubs, cafés, and whorehouses. As they drove off the following morning, Will watched them go with the first stirring of regret. He said to Mary, "Sweetheart, I'm getting a little tired of cathedrals."

"But I thought you liked them. I thought you said so."

"Of course, but aren't we here to see more? I really need to understand the French for my job." He added, "It's not as if you were a Catholic or anything."

So the itinerary changed, and they completed the circuit in the sweaty thunder of Tivoli Gardens and Place Pigalle. She loved the look of excitement on his face as they descended into the loud smoky music and steamy air; even as he shouted encouragement to her across a round table, she knew he longed for something unexpected, something that might save a little piece of himself for later.

On the night before their boat left, in a hotel in Le Havre, she surprised him with a leather box. Inside were tens of objects, pieces of ephemera from every region, every country, tourist bits like miniature landmarks and local crafts like clay figurines and fishing boats made of grass. All summer she had been collecting for this box.

She said, "It's so you remember. For your job."

She wrote: *I am trying to bring back all the bedrooms I have ever lived in. Now that I have returned to my father's house for good, it seems time to see where I went. I bought a pad of graph paper, and a plastic square, and a box of hard pencils, and I am making a plan of each, a quarter inch to the foot. This is not as hard as it sounds because, of course, I have always had that same bed, a yardstick, but now it has your scratch across the headboard, a straight fissure through the curly maple like a road cut. Some of my bedrooms are very painful to remember, like the house in Wellesley. Other than that, I don't know what I expect to learn from charting my rooms, unless it is that wide windows have always been good for me.*

They lived in Cambridge on the bottom floor of a brown-shingled two-family, not far from the consulting firm where Will analyzed international business trends. She researched butterflies and insects for *Horticulture* magazine, and on Friday afternoons, a few minutes before two, she would run across Massachusetts Avenue to stand in line for rush tickets at Symphony. Often she saw her mother-in-law arriving in her mink coat and yellow rubber boots, and occasionally curly-headed conservatory boys would ask her out for coffee.

Will looked forward to the day they would move out of their modest apartment with its too friendly Italian landlord, but Mary loved that collection of small rooms, each one with a purpose, like jewelry boxes. They owned very little furniture, but there was a built-in hutch in the dining room, a small bookcase in the parlor, a window seat and mirror in the entrance hall, a linen closet outside the bedroom, and a line of brass clothes hooks in the bedroom. She covered the pantry shelves with paper and made orderly rows of bright cans and colored boxes, and each time she went in she would think of her father's garden.

On Sundays, they liked to walk to the river, cross one bridge, then work down to the next, for a full circle that brought them home to hot tea. One Sunday, when spring had driven the last of the frost from the banks, Will said, "I just hope you're not getting bored. Don't you want to find something more to do? I don't know, ballet lessons?"

"But I'm never going to get bored. W-w-why do you ask that?"

"I just think someone as smart as you would want something more than that silly job."

The next Sunday, Mary went to church, alone. Inside the gray clapboard building there was order, and light, and flowers, and mystery, but still, she knew there would always be something missing from Will's life.

Mary kept going to church, but Will moved them to Wellesley anyway. They drove into town one night to have dinner with two other couples; he thought it would cheer her after the latest miscarriage. Waiting for them, in a French spot decorated with Paris scenes made out of soldered tin, were the Billingses, who lived on Beacon Hill, and the Blooms, who were leaving, the very next day, for Selma.

"Tell the truth, Mort," said Will. "Aren't you scared?"

"They can't wipe out a whole bus. I don't think Sylvia should go but—"

Sylvia interrupted: "Kennedy *died* for this. No one has any *choice.*"

"But," said Will, "playing the devil's advocate here, isn't this a problem for the South itself to—"

Sylvia interrupted again: "The Jews that said that are all in *ovens.*"

Mary heard this with a start. Sylvia was right, she thought, but she hadn't realized the Blooms were Jewish. It was as if that gave them something to be, something to grow into. She looked at the Billingses, silent and distracted during the discussion, and wondered why they had been invited to this gathering. Then, as she had often done around Will's hearty friends, she wondered why she had been invited. Then, as he continued to debate, preparing his voice and hesitating every time he said the word "Jew" or "Negro," she wondered why Will had been invited.

On the way home, driving out on Route 9, she could see Will chewing the inside of his cheek. Halfway, they came upon a car wreck, and there were police blinkers and the harsh light of ambulances with their doors open, and a man screaming for his wife. Mary felt empty and dark, a body that would bear no children, like their big stucco house in Wellesley, with hemlock hedges strangling every window. As they drove up the gravel driveway, Will announced, "I'm going to go. Mort and Syl are right. I'm going to Alabama."

After a few days, there was no more mention of Freedom Riding. Instead, he kept talking about that accident, the terrible arbitrariness of it, the momentary, mad collision of circumstance. For Will, the matter ended in a great black hole, but Mary, feeling the last hormones of her pregnancy forsaking her body, was not sure, not sure at all.

It probably shouldn't surprise you to hear that however much I continue to grieve for you, which is illusory, I become more whole, which is fact. My life is a crab's life, the life of a scavenger content to hack at the pieces left behind. You're looking for the meaning of breath;

I'm looking for a lost mitten. I have learned to envy your restless treasure hunt. I came to this conclusion the other day when I was working in my garden. I turned over a spade of sod that was dense with root, with seed and wildflower bulbs and tubers, and I saw a whole season of life laid out side to side, clumped and spaced, patient and forgiving. It was then I realized also how much I pitied you.

Will, at last, had been transferred to the Paris office. The assassinations and the riots at Columbia had terrified him, but the barricades of that summer in Paris gave him the quickening heady sense of being there for history. He let his hair grow well over his collar and took to wearing tight shirts with epaulets, and salmon-colored trousers. Still, when he found them an apartment, it was on the Right Bank, a peaceful untouched neighborhood just off L'Etoile, a place with wrought-iron gates and cast-iron balconies, and high narrow doors and marble stairs.

Mary stayed behind for two months to wrap up her church committee work and to sell the Wellesley house to a family of seven.

When she joined Will in their new home in Paris, she found a pair of women's underpants hanging on a brass hook behind the bathroom door. They were beige, and American-made. She pressed them into her palm, where they burned like a hot coin, and she went dizzy staring at the black-and-white tiles on the walls and floor. She had no place of her own to hide them, so she put them in her pocketbook and carried them for weeks. She spent many days at the Louvre and kept wondering if she had made fun of the silly face he made when he kissed. When the underpants became gray in the pencils, ticket stubs, and loose change of her bag, she washed them and put them in her bureau. Every time she wore them she tried to picture her.

Will bought Mary a bright mini-skirt and a see-through blouse at a boutique on the rue de Rivoli. She modeled them for him once, but never wore them outside. One day she went to lunch with a curator of Dutch paintings. He wore a cashmere suit and onyx cuff links; he seated her with a smooth assurance, ordered an aperitif with two ice cubes on the side, and snapped his long fingers at the waiter who forgot the condiments for his steak tartare. By dessert, all these stylish Continental ways had reduced her to a laughing fit, which she stifled into her napkin.

She took long train rides, slow locals to Avignon, Munich, and Amsterdam. She sat in compartments on worn seats of red velvet that smelled of babies and tarragon, and wrote thoughts in a journal. The words came out in unfamiliar voices, loaded with paradox and sudden turns she barely understood. Sometimes, when the door banged open and a businessman or a nun or a schoolgirl would slip in, she would look up in fright.

For their vacation, in the fall, they lived for a week

on a canal boat, gliding in silence through vineyards and wheat fields. The captain's heavy wife served them fresh bread and chicken, and picked on Will. It was on the boat, while they were sitting in aluminum lawn chairs on the foredeck, heading into a red sun, that Will told her about trying LSD.

"In Cambridge. With Harvey and Monica. We knew you wouldn't be interested."

"W-w-when?"

"I told you. Last winter in Cambridge."

"No. When? Where was I? W-w-where was I? Was I sitting out in that prison in W-w-w . . . oh *shit* . . . in W-w-wellesley when you and Harvey and Monica all took LSD?"

"We did it a couple of times. Three times really. Harvey and I called in sick, and it was just stupid and infantile that we had to sneak around like that."

"Oh."

He waited for her to say more. When she didn't, he said, "You really can't believe what it's like."

Mary's eyes widened.

He persisted. "The thing is, what I remember most vividly, what I understood, for the first time really, truly, was you, and how much I—"

She stood up and slapped him across the face, so hard he began to whimper, and whimper, and he took off his glasses and wiped his eyes, and the color drained from his face except for the outline of her hand, which was blue.

*   *   *

Mary in the Mountains

Would it please you to know I'm seeing someone? I'm not in love with him, just seeing him, and how I love that way of saying it. Because as much as I loved you I'm not sure I ever saw you. My dog Arnold is seeing him too, with his nose; when he comes over Arnold samples his shoes, his crotch, his trousers, and then curls up in the corner of the floor. My friend does not talk very much, although I suspect he goes home worrying that he talked my ear off. So there the three of us sit, in that fussy parlor my mother thought so elegant, in the dark of late dusk, just seeing each other.

The Billingses came to dinner to look over the new Cambridge house, but they were so busy bickering at each other they had little appetite for the veal. Harvey sprawled in a loveseat with his hands tucked deep into his waistband and his feet stacked heel-to-toe, as if everyone was supposed to admire his shoes, and from time to time he would loll his head sideways to spew insults all over his wife.

Mary kept leaving the room, but each time she did, the conversation died, as if the three of them had so exhausted each other that the only fun left was to display it to the world.

"Oh yeah, Will. Did I tell you where Monica was that other night? I can't remember if I told you this one. Hey, Mary, hey wait, let me . . ."

After an hour of this Mary turned off the stove and went to her bedroom. She put on a nightgown, brushed out her hair, graying quickly now, and felt the promise of an early fall as it parted the curtains and passed over her bed.

The morning of her forty-second birthday Will got up for work early and was gone by the time she came down. On the breakfast table he had set her place with a yellow placemat, and a folded yellow napkin, and a small blue box centered between the silver. She pushed the box aside and ate her breakfast, and all day long avoided the kitchen.

She opened it, finally, in the late afternoon. It was a string of pearls spaced with tiny gold balls, all strung on a fine golden chain. She stared at the pearls, cradled in satin, ran her fingertip down the line, and then burst into tears. Who could he have been thinking about when he bought those pearls for her? Around what young neck had he pictured them hanging?

You have asked me if I forgive you, after all these years. You should know better than to ask a Christian that question. It's like asking a poet, Is the rain a symbol for death? If the truth were that simple, the answer would have been that simple. Forgiveness has nothing to do with time and nothing to do with me. Forgiveness is a high meadow, yellow grasses surrounded by the dense, sharp tangle of spruce trees. It exists, I promise you, but it's not a place for me to go, much as I would like to. It's a place for you to find, alone.

*   *   *

"Wouldn't you like to go away for a while? Maybe find a place you can think without me moping around?"

Mary jerked her head up, startled. She was reading in her study, and from the corner of her eye the plumber's helper Will was carrying looked like a club.

He repeated: "I've just been running it over and over. And I suddenly realized how selfish I've been."

"Are you asking me to leave? Is that what you want me to do?"

"No. Not at all. It's just that lately you've seemed so worn out, and it's me, I know it's me doing this to you. So I thought you'd have fun planning some kind of trip. To Europe maybe."

"I don't think I'd have much fun in Paris, even you can see that."

"I did not mean France," he said curtly.

She reached her hand over to his hairy thigh. He was wearing only his undershorts and watch. "Will. Sit down." She gave him a slight push toward a chair. "Sit down and talk to me."

"I really don't have time for this. I didn't want a big thing."

"Is there anything wrong?"

"Wrong? I clogged the toilet." He held up the plumber's helper for her to see.

"Is everything at work okay? Everything's all straightened out?"

"What in God's name are you after? Everything's fine at work. You know that."

"Do you want me to be your friend? Is someone treating you badly? You can talk to me about it."

He blushed.

"Do you feel okay? You're not worried about any health things, are you?"

"No."

"Then there's nothing wrong," she said, and glanced back at her book.

"Well, Christ, Mary. Doesn't the world strike you as a bit peculiar? Just look out the window. Read the paper someday. You get killed these days for having a fashionable pair of sunglasses. Reagan's going to win and then you can kiss it all goodbye. The Russians are moving missiles into East Germany, the Arabs have us by the balls, and the spics, from Mexico to Tierra del Fuego, are going to self-destruct, except they'll take us and our economy with them. I've never understood why all your church stuff makes you miss these little details. Next time you're on your knees I really wish you'd think about this."

"I have noticed that the world is not a kind or generous place. That's what I think about when, as you say, I'm on my knees."

"But you don't think about me, do you?"

"I thought you said nothing is wrong with you."

"Jesus, Mary. How can you be so cruel? You're just so goddamn *cruel*." His mouth quivered and tears flooded his eyes.

She reached out again for his knees, but he bolted up and ran out into the hall, where he let out a yelp, like a dog. He was still carrying the plumber's helper, and a few minutes later Mary heard a great rush of water as the toilet ran free again.

On Wednesday, or Thursday, if Wednesday is rainy or bitter cold, I take my neighbor Violet for a walk. She is not much past seventy, but she says living in the same house all her life has given her arthritis and she leans very heavily on me. She would like to go out more often, but I have to take a rest between outings. Violet has never been outside the state of New Hampshire, which is fine with her really, but she loves to hear about other places and wonders if she would have the courage to climb what she calls the Iffel Tour. As we walk, picking our way around tricky stones and across frozen ruts, so entwined it's hard to know which of the four legs are the bad ones, I tell her my stories. I'm sure by now most of what I say is plain fiction, but she doesn't care. When I repeat myself, she starts jabbing a deformed knuckle into my side to urge me to get on to the parts she loves, about trains, and about people who fear for their souls. She sighs happily when I close out a chapter, as if there is now music, and sometimes, on the sad but replete close, Violet says, That was lovely. Along the way she has formed a very firm picture of you, and even though I have never told her anything severe, she tenses when you come on stage and gives you a villain's hiss. She is Catholic, though, and says rosaries for you. She wants me to convert so I can drive her to Mass. I tell her to go to hell and we both laugh, two ladies with the vague fear we're going there anyway.

Mary's father died a few months after his eightieth birthday, and left the house to Mary. A few months later, she and Will packed most of her portable things into their cars, and they drove up from Boston into the mountains in a convoy. Will insisted they stop in Concord for a "nice lunch," and Mary sat in a renovated mill building and pictured them eating ice cream together, thirty years earlier. She could not understand why, with everything that had happened since, she didn't want this breakup.

After they had unloaded the cars she began to ache, a hollow tightness she hadn't felt in years. Will waited in the mudroom while she cried softly and briefly; then they kissed and he was gone. The old forester's woolen pants and mackintosh still hung on the pegs of the mudroom, with a sprig of fir stuck in one pocket. Six pairs of boots, one for each working day, stood in a line, and the last pair was still caked in mud.

The house smelled faintly of lavender and cedar, her mother's presence decades after her death, and of woodsmoke and dogs, her father's. In the dark parlor, upholstered in English linen with camelbacks and ball-and-claw feet, she found the row of Staffordshire her mother had collected: the chimney sweep, the happy milkmaid, the sea captain home for good.

She walked into her father's study, with its rows of Kipling, Gibbon, and Tennyson, its Loeb classics, its Zane Grey and Bret Harte. In the corner was a pile of Christmas novels, most from her and all, how it pleased her, unread. On the desk was the last manuscript of a forestry handbook that would never be published. She rubbed the desk surface and smelled her father's chalky forearms on her hands, and knelt down to kiss the permanent shape in the leather of his chair.

She wrote: *It is a paradox I cannot escape that you, who believe the world has been so uniquely damaged by the modern age, are still capable of the deepest faith, while I, who find the Holy Ghost in even the most hideous and ardent acts, will always be among the children at the gates. Faith is the assurance of things hoped for, the conviction of things not seen. You, on your treasure hunt that has caused me such pain, have held hopes beyond madness, and you have stared at the unseen so long that your eyes are hollow. Your thirst, that sandy being I used to feel in bed with me, turning your blood to powder and your flesh to bone, will save you.*

She wrote: *If you send me a picture of your son I will put it on my bureau. It was kind of you to write and not just send an announcement, although an announcement is more than I would have expected. The joy, at*

Christopher Tilghman

your age, to have a child at last. But please don't think his picture will be alone on my bureau. Please don't think yours is the only face I see in the branches of oak trees. I've never lost anyone. That is what will save me. The memories are my grace, and all of you, as you can hear me say, are w-w-welcome in my heart.